RETURNING HOME

Returning Home

CHRISTIE MACDONALD

Returning Home (Darlings Lake Series, Book 1)

Published by Nova Hope Publishing
Summerville, Nova Scotia
NovaHopePublishing.com

ASIN: B0G6XJ9ZNP
ISBN: 978-1-0674098-2-1(ebook)
ISBN: 978-1-0674098-0-7 (Paperback)
ISBN: ISBN 978-1-0674098-1-4 (Hardcover)

This novel, my first ever, is dedicated to Megan and Mia, my first true loves. You bring me so much joy and I am continuously thankful that I get to be your mom.

To Brian- Yesterday, Today, Tomorrow, Forever. I love you.

Foreward

Christie Macdonald has been a dear friend of mine for twenty-two years now. From the first day we met, I was struck by her charisma, enthusiasm, and incredible sense of humor. Everything Christie puts her mind to, she does with excellence- and this novel is no exception.

Returning Home follows Sadie Campbell's journey through complicated relationships, unexpected romance, and the ache of unmet expectations. As you read, you may recognize glimpses of your own life in her struggles, and in her discoveries. That's what happened for me.

Christie has this rare gift for putting into words the feelings many of us carry but can hardly express. Her writing is honest, healing, and full of heart; gently guiding readers toward understanding, compassion, and their own version of returning home.

This book is more than a story- it invites you to explore parts of your heart and mind that maybe you haven't faced before. It reminds us that our past, and our mistakes do not define us, and that God can bring beauty from ashes, even when life doesn't go as planned.

Read with an open heart, and this book may change how you see life, and yourself.

-Jessica Hudson, Recording Artist & ECMA Nominee

"For I know the plans I have for you, declares the Lord,
plans to prosper you and not to harm you,
plans to give you hope and a future."

Jeremiah 29:11

Chapter One

Now

In the middle of September under a cluster of gorgeous and colorful maple trees, Sadie Campbell sat in the driver's seat of her parked SUV, watching the leaves slowly fall and rest on the windshield. She had pulled into her church parking lot ten minutes earlier and backed into a spot where the mature trees provided coverage from the setting sun. With a freshly mowed lawn and fallen leaves scattered over nearby picnic tables, the parking lot of her church could have easily passed for one found in a provincial park. Emily Lopez, her best friend since elementary school, had asked Sadie to join her here this evening, emphasizing that it would mean the world to her if she'd come. Sadie rolled down her window so she could feel the light breeze and watched for Emily's little green Volkswagen to pull into the parking lot.

Though she had known about this meeting for a few weeks now, Sadie had not been looking forward to attending, even with Emily by her side, and had procrastinated in getting ready. By the time her parents had arrived at the house to watch her kids, Sadie had decided it would be fine to just wear what she had on when they'd arrived. Looking down at her outfit now, she wondered if she should have made more of an effort.

As the owner of the most successful photography agency in the province, and possibly in the country, she generally spent time and effort on her appearance before leaving the house. And while she had a partiality to dressing comfortably, she also preferred to look put-together and rarely left the house in what she was wearing now- snug fitting ankle-length jeans- ripped at the knees, her favorite grey University of Toronto hoodie that had a large navy emblem across the chest, and cuffs so tattered around the wrists that her thumbs could slip through the two holes she had worn through the material. The oversized hoodie enveloped her small frame, it was one she normally only wore around her home at the end of a long day or saved for lazy weekends. She did have on brand new sneakers, which she hoped offered some style points, but they were still not enough to stop her from second-guessing her overall choice of attire. She leaned her head back against the headrest and realized that between her outfit choice and her long brown hair pulled back in a loose ponytail, she probably looked more like a teenager than the 32 years that she was. People would probably wonder why she was there tonight.

Sadie's cellphone chimed in the custom text tone Emily had programmed into it. Looking at it now, Sadie saw that Emily would 'Be there in 2 Minutes!'. Emily knew that Sadie was a planner by nature and knew she would be starting to get nervous wondering where Emily was. Sadie smiled at her phone and once again thanked God for Emily's friendship, something she did often.

Since Sadie had been very young, she had thrived in environments when she knew what the plan was and what was going to be happening next. Her mother, Caroline Campbell, had once told her that Sadie used to ask her every day on their drives into her elementary school, *'What's the plan for today? What are we having for supper? Do we have plans tonight? Is anyone coming over for a visit? Do we need to go anywhere?'* She shared that Sadie had always relaxed once Caroline was able to walk her through the day, no matter what it looked like. Sadie's need for wanting to know what the plan was continued into her teenage years and through to adulthood. While quirky to some, Sadie knew that her need to have a plan had benefited her in many ways.

As a teenager, as part of her Sunday routine, Sadie would sit at the desk in her bedroom and use her favorite colored pens, pencils, stickers and stationary to plan out what her week would look like, making sure she had color-coded in her school agenda specific times each day for homework, or to study when she knew she had upcoming tests or exams. She blocked time for youth group at her church, for sports tryouts and then for practices when she had them. She made sure she had time scheduled in her week to hang out with friends, watch her favorite TV shows so she wouldn't miss them, and she even scheduled time on Sundays to create the next week's plan. Her planning and organizational skills had not only given Sadie a sense of comfort, but it allowed her to focus her attention on where she was and who she was with. She rarely wondered if she should be somewhere else or doing something else. This was a character trait that as she got older others often commented on because it was so rare and so appreciated. Over time, instead of weekly plans, Sadie began to experiment with monthly and yearly plans, and when she found that beneficial, she used the same process to take the large personal, business, financial, and health goals that she had and break them into bite-sized pieces, ensuring she had given herself enough time to meet each of the targets she set for herself. Now, whenever someone asks her how she's managed so much professional growth at such a young age, she credits her love of planning and setting small achievable goals.

She reached for the wallet-sized calendar she kept in her bag and pulling it out and flipping it open, was about to go through her plan for the week when she saw Emily's car turn into the parking lot. Taking a deep breath, Sadie placed her calendar back in her bag. She picked up her bag which held her schedule, wallet, keys and phone and placed it behind her, on the floor behind the passenger seat. Much to her father's chagrin, Sadie had always considered this an effective way to keep her belongings safe.

Stephen Campbell, a police officer by trade, was with her a few years earlier when she followed her bag-in-the-backseat routine. 'I don't like locking my car,' she had shared with him when he asked her what she was doing. 'I just want to get into it when I need to without having to rummage through my bag looking for my keys.' When her father had begun to protest Sadie had continued, 'Don't worry dad! Everyone in a small town knows moving your bag to the backseat is the universal signal for 'No, you can't take it. What's in there is important- it's why it's placed out of sight.'

He had then proceeded to take Sadie's keys out of her bag, lock the car for her, and toss the keys in her direction.

She and her dad spoke of Sadie's theory on backseat theft often.

Sadie got out of her car and began to walk towards Emily, who had parked a few spots away from her and was also placing her bag on the floor of her back seat. After getting out of her car and shutting the car door behind her, she offered her best friend a tentative smile- simultaneously offering support while also trying to gauge how Sadie was feeling. Sadie pulled her sweater tighter and thought about the irony of it all- of being here tonight, with Emily, at this church, and for this meeting.

For as much as making plans and schedules had served Sadie, she had also learned through experience that there would be times that unexpected events would occur, plans would change. She had practice in pivoting, refocusing, in modifying her initial timelines and expectations. A soccer practice would get cancelled, a final exam would get moved up, a flat tire on a road trip extended her ETA by hours, her son ran a fever just as she was supposed to leave for a business trip, a work contract wasn't signed as expected, or, two great photography opportunities arrived at once- for the same time frame in two different locations. For most of her life Sadie felt confident that though she was an experienced planner, her real success came in her unmatched ability to redefine the next steps after an unexpected circumstance.

But that was then.

Sadie was meeting Emily here tonight because Sadie's planning and goal-setting processes were no longer working for her, and they hadn't been for a long time. Because Sadie had never planned to have her heart broken, twice. That wasn't on any plan. At 25 she hadn't planned to call her mom, the woman she looked up to the most, to tell her with a racing heart and no longer able to hide the tears, that her marriage wasn't the same as her parents- that it wasn't strong or healthy, and that she was so sad, so embarrassed, so... lost.

That wasn't on a list.

And as a young girl, nowhere had she written among her personal goals in colored cursive writing, that as an adult when she had children at home, she would walk into her childhood church, encouraged by her childhood best friend, to attend DivorceCare because her best friend knew how much she needed it. No, she hadn't had aspirations of that. And yet, here she was.

Slowly walking across the parking lot towards the church entrance, Emily watched Sadie quietly processing. Knowing her better than anyone, and sensing her starting to internally spiral, she looped her arm through Sadie's and held her close.

"We're going in together, Sade. I'm really proud of you."

Sadie squeezed Emily back, thankful for her friend's un-wavering confidence and strength.

'*Oh Sadie, if only you knew,*' Emily thought with the clear-est conviction, '*Tonight is going to change everything.*'

Chapter Two

Then

Sadie had lived in Darlings Lake, Nova Scotia for most of her life, the exception being four years following her High School graduation when she lived in Toronto to attend university and complete her bachelor's degree in visual arts.

She was the oldest daughter of Caroline and Stephen Campbell, a couple who had been excited to be transferred to Darlings from Manitoba when they were in their mid-twenties. The transfer followed a difficult assignment for Stephen, who was a member of the Royal Canadian Mounted Police. They looked forward to a slower pace in a small town where the crime rate was low and the community was welcoming. The National Accounting and Relocation agent that had been assigned to the Campbells had helped them find a small two-bedroom cottage nestled on a beautiful lakefront property on the outskirts of town. The home was hidden from the road and the gravel driveway leading to the property was lined with full sized maple trees, a scenic view from the outset. Despite the advanced warning they had received that the cottage needed some love, when they walked into the space for the first time and Caroline saw the wooden floors, exposed wooden beams, and rustic decor left by the previous owner, she knew immediately that this was going to be their home. It was the first home either of them had owned and together, they couldn't have been more thrilled. In her first scan of the living room, she noted with appreciation the large windows with a view of the lake, but more importantly, she immediately knew where she would place their Christmas tree.

As a constable in a small town, Stephen worked often and Caroline and Stephen had agreed that instead of focusing on building a career, Caroline would stay home and volunteer at their local church and in their community until God blessed them with children. A year after they settled into Darlings, Caroline discovered she was pregnant and had wept from the joy of it, after having tried unsuccessfully to become pregnant for years beforehand. Sadie was their first born, arriving that July both healthy and heavy, and with Caroline so focused on loving on Sadie, it wasn't for many months into her second pregnancy until she realized that God had blessed them again. The day after Sadie's second birthday Scarlett joined their family, a beautiful little sister for Sadie and from day one Sadie had doted on her, squeezing her too tight and kissing her too hard. With their hearts overflowing with gratitude, Caroline and Stephen committed to raising the girls to know and love the Lord.

Sadie grew up to be an active child, playing soccer and attending a local Christian camp through her summers. From a young age she had enjoyed school and spent significant amounts of time on her schoolwork and homework through the school year. When Sadie was seven, halfway through the school year, her grade one teacher Mrs. Hamilton, had stood at the front of their class next to a little girl that nobody recognized and announced that a new family had recently moved to town and that 'Emily here, is going to be joining our class'. In front of everyone Mrs. Hamilton asked Sadie if at recess she wouldn't mind showing Emily around the school, and Sadie, feeling shy, but also excited about the potential of a new friend, nodded that she would.

Though she loved to be active, Sadie had been a naturally quiet child and while she had some friends from her church, she had struggled to find friends in her class at school. Sadie realized quickly that Emily wasn't shy at all, and Emily talked to Sadie the whole time they walked through the school and around the playground. She told Sadie right away that she loved her Strawberry Shortcake sweater and offered to let Sadie use her skip-it when she pulled it from her bookbag. Once Emily showed Sadie how to use it, she told Sadie how her dad was a policeman too! She talked to Sadie about what it was like being an only child, about the town they had just moved from- it sounded so different from Darlings Lake, and what it was like to pack up all of your toys and put them in a box and move to a new house and into a new bedroom in a new town. Sadie couldn't imagine it. From that first day Emily had made friendship easy, and in the more than 20 years that they'd been friends, that had never changed.

The Campbells remained involved in their church and each week while her parents were in the main service, the girls attended Sunday School. Sadie and Scarlett both loved church and felt welcomed there. It was almost like having a whole second family. When the girls got older and aged out of Sunday school, they moved into the sanctuary where the adults sat to hear the Pastor's sermon. On Sunday mornings the teenagers all sat together in the back row and on Wednesday evenings, the same group of kids, plus other kids from school that didn't come to church on Sundays, attended Youth Group at the same church. Emily had always turned down Sadie and Scarlett's invitations for her to join them on Sundays, but that changed the year they were old enough for Youth Group, when Emily found herself with a crush on a boy who came to youth on Wednesday nights. Sadie didn't care what reason Emily had to say yes to coming to church, she was just glad she had started to come. Caroline and Stephen picked Emily up each week and it eventually got to the point that if the Campbells were out of town, Emily would find her own ride to church- Sundays and Wednesdays.

Sadie hadn't been allowed to date until she was 16, a rule she hadn't even noticed. Focused on hanging out with friends and her own extra-curricular activities, she hadn't thought about boys in any significant way until the summer before she began High School. That was the summer she had spent her vacation working with one of her best friends, Mason Gray at the same Christian camp that they had attended as children.

When the Campbells had moved to Darlings, Mason's mom Judy was the first person to show up on their doorstep to welcome Caroline and Stephen to town, offering Caroline a warm pie and an even warmer hug. Living next to each other, the Campbell and Gray families became close, frequently visiting each other's homes for coffee and conversation, and celebrating exciting life events with each other, including pregnancies, new births, and holiday seasons. Caroline and Judy reared their children together, giving each other a break by taking the other's children when one only had planned a trip to the local park or beach.

Mason and Sadie were in the same grade and because of the closeness of their parents, had grown up together. They shared the same faith in God and Mason was the boy that Sadie knew she could talk to about anything. It was natural for Judy to walk by Mason's bedroom only to find Sadie in there with him, hanging out on his bed, listening to music, and going through his CD collection. Mason was one of the two people Sadie would call first when she had something exciting to share, or when she had something on her mind that was bothering her, and she wanted to talk it through. Emily was the other. She loved and trusted them both.

On the day Sadie received her grade nine report card, advising her that she had met all of the criteria required to graduate from Junior High and move into grade 10 at the High School, Sadie's parents held a special dinner for her and Scarlett, who had also received a report card that day confirming she had completed the requirements of her grade seven year. Following dinner, when the dishes had been cleared and the kitchen cleaned, her parents invited Sadie into the living room. It was on that evening that her parents gifted her with a Canon EOS Rebel, a beautiful camera that Sadie had secretly been both longing and saving for. Sadie screamed when she opened it, threw her arms tightly around her father's neck, and then her mother's. Opening the camera box and staring at the camera in awe, she asked her parent's permission to leave and go show Mason. Her parents happily obliged and Sadie took off for the Gray's.

Running up the stairs and busting into Mason's room, out of breath and with a huge smile on her face, Sadie held up the camera. Mason sat up on his bed, where he had just settled in to start reading 'Harry Potter and the Philosopher's Stone' a novel that had only been released on the previous day, and to critical acclaim. (He was very surprised to receive it as a gift from his parents that evening, who had waited in line to buy it for him knowing how much he loved reading. He was also very confident that they were unaware that the book revolved around a school of wizards, but he wasn't about to tell them that and give them something frivolous to worry about).

He put his book down and grinned at her as he listened to her talk his ear off about the different functions of the camera and how long it should take for her to study the manual and figure out how it worked. With no other plan other than reading a book that would be there when he got back, Mason offered to walk with Sadie through the path in the woods behind their homes- the one that joined their backyards together, so that she could test out some of the different camera features. Sadie loved that idea and without asking his permission, grabbed his favorite white worn sweater that was draped over the back of his desk chair. In her excitement to show Mason her camera, she had forgotten to grab one of her own sweaters and trotting down the stairs with him she threw it on, the sweater ending just above her knees, the sleeves reaching her fingertips.

Walking quietly next to Mason through his backyard, she held tightly to the new camera that hung around her neck. Heading towards the point where his lawn ended and the wooded path began, she found herself thanking God for His many blessings. Another school year was behind her, she was on the cusp of a summer that included working at a camp she loved, she had really good friends and a family she adored, and now she had a means to practice a hobby that had always brought her joy. She felt truly content, like this was exactly where she was meant to be.

Chapter Three

Then

When Mason's dad John Gray, was in his mid-30's he had been fishing for lobster off the coast of Southwest Nova Scotia for almost two decades. Knowing that the hard work and physical labour was taking a toll on his body, he started to look for ways he might be able to make money in the industry without having to spend his days and nights on the water.

Following the close of the lobster season in May, John began researching different types of bait, other than fresh fish, that captains could use to catch lobster. Bait was an ongoing and costly expense. It was time-consuming and labour intensive to prepare fresh fish for traps, and John knew if he could somehow design artificial bait that was good for the environment, saved captains thousands of dollars on operating costs and also enticed lobster at the same rate as real raw fish, he would be in business. After much trial and error and quiet testing by his friends, six different designs later his patent application was approved and he opened a small business developing artificial lobster bait made from everything from rubber to stainless steel, each product able to hold the scents of baitfish and shellfish that lobster are naturally drawn to.

Environmental sustainability was not a common concept at that time, nor was it a priority of the various government agencies John had needed funding from to get his company up and off the ground. After being declined for small business grants from each agency they applied to, John and Judy used their own savings to invest in themselves. They registered the business name 'Gray's Gear', and that business purchased the smallest fishing shanty on the largest fishing wharf in Darlings, along with enough material to build 1,000 products, or approximately enough to provide two boats with a season's worth of bait.

Even though his business was first met with skepticism from local businessmen, captains kept a close eye on how John's friends made out using the new bait. Fishermen are infamous for their superstitions and sticking to what they know works, so while no one was interested in starting a season by switching their bait to a relatively new and untested product, John knew that once they heard whispers that his buddies continued to catch lobster while saving money over the season, that they would become interested as well.

And that is exactly what happened.

A few years after the local fishermen began buying Gray's products, word spread internationally as fishermen took well deserved vacations and travelled to different locations around the world, sharing with friends their successes of the season.

Within only two years of local fisherman buying John's artificial lobster lures, Gray's Gears began receiving calls from captains across Canada, and from fishing captains in the United States, Australia, New Zealand, from several Caribbean nations, and from captains in South Africa, Ireland, France and Italy. Through the years John received many calls from Private Equity firms across the United States and the United Kingdom looking to buy his company, and John, while always flattered and sometimes shocked, after praying for guidance always ended up politely declining the offers. His intention was to raise his children to learn the business and when John could see that Mason was ready to not only handle, but thrive with such an immense amount of responsibility, he planned to pass his business along to his first-born son. If at that time Mason wanted to sell, he would leave that to him, but it was important for John to be able to someday hand over to Mason the business he and his wife had grown from the ground up.

Due to the success of John's business, which was now internationally acclaimed within the lobster industry, he had had no choice but to expand. While a new, much larger warehouse was built on the oceanfront near the wharf, and a full team was hired to run the various aspects of his operations, John kept his very first shanty on the wharf as his primary office. It reminded him of where his business had started.

His work was constantly interrupted by fishermen coming and going delivering coffee and donuts at all hours of the day, all with a yarn to spin. Even when he left his office smelling like fish, and despite Judy's gentle nudging when she did the laundry, he refused to work out of anywhere else. He wouldn't change a thing. He was a man who laughed every single day.

When Gray's Gear financial statements showed stable growth and increased profits year after year, John and Judy never bought a new house. They stayed in their own cottage by the lake next to the Campbells and never upgraded their vehicle until it was required.

Other than sizable donations to their church and causes they cared about, the Gray's had never demonstrated in any way how financially well-off they actually were. John had always told his three children, Mason, Jenny, and Liam, that living in a small town had more perks than not, and that in his experience, being a good neighbor and a loyal friend was a reward in and of itself. Sometimes though, he knew from experience that being kind to others can pay dividends in ways that one wouldn't expect or anticipate.

Chapter Four

Then

Mason Gray turned 15 at the beginning of June during his last year of Junior High. He and his dad had spent the previous three years tinkering away and slowly restoring an antique car that John had been gifted years earlier. The two spent many evenings and weekends together in the garage, classic rock playing on a workbench radio, while John taught Mason the mechanics of how the car worked, and Mason, loving the time with his dad, took the time to listen and learn. It was also a chance for Mason to hear about his dad's business and ask him questions about the ins-and-outs of that as well.

Months before John received the car, he had been praying and asking God to show him new ways that he could connect with his son. Mason had just turned 12; he was getting older and had begun wanting to spend more time alone, or with friends, than he did with John. John learned of the generous gift following a call he received from Sarah Bredon, a woman who lived in Shelburne, the next town over. Sarah was the only child of Thomas Bredon Sr. (Tommy to most), a Cape Breton native and great friend to John. She had called to let John know that her dad had become very ill and asked if it would be possible for John to come visit her dad that week. John said absolutely he would, and he and Sarah spent some time talking on the phone about her dad and the history of their friendship.

John spoke with Sarah of Tommy's love of hot coffee and honey crullers and he told Sarah that he rarely saw the man without two of each, a pair for himself, and a pair for John, jokingly adding that many years ago he had had to join a gym because of her dad. Sarah laughed and then shared that a few nights ago, when her dad wasn't feeling particularly well and was extra sentimental, he asked her to sit with him and reminded her that should his illness take a turn, she didn't need to worry about him. He had wanted to talk to her about how he had come to know Jesus.

Tommy had then shared with his daughter a story that she had never heard, of a time over a decade prior when Tommy was in his seventies and still a crew member on the back of a boat that he worked on all his life. At the end of one of those long days when the lobsters were all unloaded, he had been crawling up the ladder that brought him from the boat to the wharf, and John had been standing there, waiting for him at the top.

John had immediately been able to recall that night. He had been watching Tommy work through the window in his shanty, marveling at the older man's resilience and determination to keep up with the young crew. His long white beard and slightly slower pace the only identifiers of Tommy's age. When Tommy reached the wharf, John had helped Tommy off the ladder and asked him to join him in his office. He then privately asked Tommy how he was feeling. John had recognized how much strength it took to haul and carry traps and the energy that it took to keep the hours that Tommy had been keeping. When Tommy reluctantly admitted to him that yes, he had been having a hard time, John immediately offered him a new job with his company, one with a generous salary and that would switch him from long shifts to regular daytime hours. The role would keep him off the water as well, he would be warm and dry for as long as he wanted to continue working. John remembered that once Tommy had processed his offer, he slowly lowered himself into the closest chair, held his head in his hands and silently wept.

After letting him have his moment, John told him not to get too excited, that he had a particular job in mind for him. He wanted Tommy to be his VP of Employee and Captain Relations, a new position at Gray's Gear. With a very generous budget, he would be responsible for ensuring John's staff had what they needed to do their jobs well including regular coffee and donut deliveries. He was to provide advice and guidance when his team had specific industry-related questions, which many of the young ones did, and when he felt an employee wasn't performing as expected, he wanted Tommy to discreetly let John know so that he could handle it. When everyone on the staff was good, he continued, he wanted Tommy to travel, wherever he needed to, to spend time with captains talking through ideas they had of what else Gray's Gear could be developing to help lower their expenses or make their work more efficient. It was a job that unbeknownst to Tommy, John had made up on the spot, but one that through the years had paid unmeasurable dividends.

Tommy became John's favorite employee. They spent hours talking about everything from fishing to family and everything in between- religion, international news, business, politics and always about John's strong faith in God. Tommy never took advantage of John's kindness. He worked as hard for John as he had for his captain on the boat, updating John on progress in the warehouse and bringing him new ideas from fishing captains. In the very first week after he started working for John, Tommy had walked into John's office with a young kid by the scruff of the neck- letting John know that he had found him- this new employee on his first day, taking pictures of files he shouldn't have been looking at. Tommy had grabbed the kid's phone and walked him from the warehouse where he was caught, all the way to the Shanty, cursing at him the whole time for his stupidity and disrespect- never letting go of the collar of his shirt.

John had told the kid to take a seat and while the kid rubbed at his neck, John went through the pictures on the phone Tommy had handed over. Tommy blocked the exit and stood with his arms crossed as John deleted all the pictures and then checked to see if they had been sent to anyone, relieved to find they hadn't been. When he was done, he talked to the kid about the importance of trust, loyalty and how decisions that you make determine consequences. As the kid started talking about how sorry he was, Tommy came up behind him, picked him up out of his chair, opened the door to the Shanty, and threw him outside yelling 'Get out of here! YOU'RE FIRED!'. When Tommy slammed the door behind him and turned back around, John had looked at him with raised eyebrows, and Tommy returned the look, looking at John as if he had three heads.

"What? I need to follow my gut boss, and that kid is trouble. And now that he knows about trust and whatever, he can also know that you're no fool!"

Tommy and John taught each other important lessons, John reiterating to Tommy what 'discreetly' meant, and Tommy teaching John how not to be taken advantage of. That incident, as it turned out, probably saved John more money through the years than he would ever have known. It had triggered the need for increased security measures, a process which Tommy also led.

The week of Sarah's call, John and his friend Jordan drove to see Sarah and Tommy, who was now in a hospital bed. Tommy took the opportunity to tell John everything that he had meant to him, to thank him for leading him to Jesus, and John had an opportunity to thank Tommy for his work, for his friendship and for teaching him how to properly fire someone.

Through fits of laughter and coughing, Tommy told John that it would mean a lot to him for John to accept the gift of his 1965 candy-apple-red convertible Ford Mustang. He conceded to John that he hadn't always cared for it like he should have, and acknowledged that it needed a lot of work, but said he thought it might be a nice project for him and Mason, something they could work on together. Tommy reminding John that sooner than it seemed, Mason was going to be able to drive. John had not known Tommy owned a car like that and when he saw it later that day he fell in love. Walking around it, he thanked God for Tommy and for using him to answer his prayer of how he could spend more time with Mason. Much like God had used John to answer Tommy's prayers so many years ago.

John knew how much work it would take to bring the old beauty back to life and wanted nothing more than to do that work with his son.

Tommy had passed away two weeks later, at eighty-seven years old, and John knew that his friendship was one he would carry with him always.

In all of the hours that Mason spent working on the car with his dad, he had never sat in the driver's seat and had never dared to ask his dad if one day he would be able to drive it. He didn't think he could stand to hear his dad say that no, he couldn't drive this one but that someday Mason could find, fix and drive one of his own. His dad had not mentioned the idea of Mason driving either, so it had remained an unspoken hope.

On Mason's 15th birthday, the year he would begin studying for his driver's license, and three years after the car had first shown up in their driveway, John called Mason outside to the garage. He had been leaning against his work bench and was looking at the beautiful and completely restored convertible Mustang. The car looked to be in perfect condition now, and as Mason stared at it with his dad, John looked over at his son, who was almost as tall as him now.

"She's a beauty." John began.

"She is." Mason responded. He had loved spending the time working with his Dad, he was bummed the project was over.

"What do you think about taking her out on the road once you get your license?"

Mason's head spun to look at his dad. "Are you serious?"

His dad chuckled. "Yeah, bud. Absolutely. You've put in as much time on this old girl as me. You've done great work. I know you'll take care of her and be a responsible driver."

"Dad! Yes! YES!" Mason couldn't stop his smile as he turned and grabbed his dad, wrapping him in a bear hug. Quickly letting him go, Mason jogged around the car to open the driver's side door. With the new understanding that he was going to be allowed to drive it, he sat in the driver's seat laughing as he imagined the feel of the steering wheel under his hands as the car came alive on the highway.

Once the adrenaline had settled and his dad had given him another hug and gone back inside, Mason jogged through the woods and over to Sadie's house to tell her the news. She stood in her kitchen in her matching pajamas and messy bun and squealed in excitement knowing how much time Mason had spent working on the car with his dad. She had heard him talk endlessly hoping that one day he'd be able to drive it.

Standing next to Mason she asked if he thought whether maybe she'd be allowed to go for a ride in it too. He stopped to think about her question. He hadn't even thought of asking his dad because to Mason, that had been a given. Whenever he'd worked on the car and let himself imagine someday driving it along the coast, Sadie had always been right there in the passenger seat next to him. The sudden realization had taken him by surprise, and with his heart rate suddenly out of rhythm, Mason tried to mask the confusion of his feelings by simply replying that 'Yeah Sade, I'm sure that would be ok'.

Chapter Five

Then

It was a month after Mason's 15th birthday when Sadie had received her new camera and she and Mason walked together along the wooded path between their homes, Sadie still holding tightly to her new gift. Neither of them were in a rush, and along the walk, Mason pointed out to Sadie different elements in the forest that he thought would be cool pictures for her to take- scraped tree bark just above their heads, baby plants with hidden berries, leaf and flower buds in various stages of their unfurling. Sadie took all of his suggestions, focusing her attention on those places that without him she might have overlooked. Marveling at how amazing nature was, she stopped to take a picture of the wooden bench that years ago their dads had placed just off the path, so that it was overlooking the pond. They had wanted to create a place where the kids could sit and watch the tadpoles and frogs.

As Sadie kneeled down to take a picture of the bench from a lower angle, she pulled his sweater up off the ground, not wanting to get it dirty, and then paused to adjust the optical zoom. Once she had the camera set where she wanted it, she pulled it closer to her eye. Focusing the camera on the bench, she casually asked Mason, "Do you ever stop and wonder how people can smell pine, see flowers budding, hear the wind rustling through the trees, feel the crunch of leaves under their feet and *still* not recognize that it was God who created it all? I just don't get it."

She took a couple of pictures and when she didn't hear him respond she turned around. She found him standing there, hands in his pockets, leaning against a tree. Without a second thought, she quickly brought the camera into focus and took his picture.

And then, for the first time since they had known each other, Sadie felt embarrassed. Her cheeks instantly warmed as they both heard the sound of the mechanical shutter click, confirming that the picture had been taken. She felt like she had been caught red-handed, initiating an intimate moment that neither of them had expected. He didn't say anything, and she did her best to shake it off.

They continued walking and she began talking extra fast about what Scarlett was up to, other places she wanted to take pictures, and about how she had to get home to start to pack for camp. She didn't let him get a word in edgewise, lest he mention her taking his picture and she was relieved to finally see the end of the path in sight. As they reached the edge of her property, she quickly thanked him for coming with her and said she had to get inside. Mason told her goodnight, said that it was no problem at all- that he would see her in a couple of days at camp, and then turned to walk back toward his house.

Sadie was still humiliated as she walked through her backyard, inside her house, down the hall and straight to the room she shared with Scarlett. Thankfully her sister wasn't home, so she had some privacy. She lay on her bed, still in Mason's sweater, and stared at her ceiling asking herself why she would have ever taken that picture. *So stupid.*

After a few more minutes of feeling sorry for herself, she rolled onto her side, picked up her camera and started flipping through the different pictures she had taken that evening. She was thinking of what a good eye Mason had to point out the different types of foliage when she landed on the picture of him, the one that had caused her so much embarrassment. The one that had ruined her evening. She planned to just delete it and forget about it altogether, but then there was something about the picture that gave her pause.

She brought the camera closer to her face and zoomed in on Mason's. Her cheeks began warming again as she looked more closely at the photograph, but this time warming for a different reason. Looking at the picture now, she could see how Mason had been looking at her when she had spontaneously taken it. He had looked thoughtful. He was looking at her in admiration, she noticed now. Like there was no one else in the world that he ever wanted to look at.

Chapter Six

Now

As Sadie and Emily came to the end of the parking lot and started up the couple of steps that would bring them into the church, Sadie was surprised to feel such familiarity approaching the entry. After not attending this church for the last three years, or any other church for that matter, she thought that she would feel like an outsider, a foreigner in a building that at one time had felt as familiar as a second home. But she didn't feel that way, and as Emily opened the door for them, Sadie was overtaken with a feeling of nostalgia.

Sadie felt Emily give her another quick squeeze, reminding her friend that she was right here with her. She looked over at Emily to acknowledge the sentiment but was shocked to see Emily not as she was moments earlier, but instead she saw Emily at 15, in glasses and braces and wearing a Boyz II Men t-shirt and jean shorts. Sadie shook her head. Emily had been 15 when she had first agreed to come to church with Sadie after Sadie had been asking her for so long to 'please come'. That night Emily had walked into the church with Sadie, holding her arm in the same way Sadie was holding hers now. Sadie thought that Emily had probably been feeling as nervous and unsure that night as Sadie was feeling tonight, not really knowing what to expect. *And hadn't God used that step of faith to change Emily's life?*

"Sadie, are you ok?" Emily was watching her with concern, "You don't look so good."

Sadie blinked again and saw her friend as she was today. "I'm sorry, yeah. Yeah, I'm ok..." She gave her head another quick shake and looked again at Emily. "It was the weirdest thing. I had...déjà vu maybe? I was just thinking about you at 15 when you first came to this church with me."

Emily chuckled, "Man, that was *so* long ago."

"I know. It's crazy." She continued, "Do you remember feeling nervous?" Sadie was honestly curious. They had been coming to church together for so long now. She didn't think that as adults they'd ever gone back and talked about how it had felt for her.

Emily thought about it for a sec. "Yeah," she replied nonchalantly, "Yeah, I'm sure I was nervous, BUT, do you know what made it easier?"

Sadie smiled knowing what was coming, "Having me there with you?"

"What!?" Emily snickered, "No! Jake was going that night!"

An unexpected laugh burst out of Sadie. "Ah... Jake Johnson." Emily's teenage crush.

"Yes! He was so hot!" Emily joined in Sadie's laughter. "Back then he and Mason were inseparable."

"Yeah, they were." Sadie's laugh faded as she thought about Mason, something she had been actively working on *not* doing.

Looking ahead, the women saw the registration table and the reminder of why they were here settled back over them. "Can you give me just a minute, Em? I just want to collect my thoughts before I go register."

"Yes, of course babe, no problem." Emily nodded ahead and told Sadie that she would just be over there talking to the women working the registration desk, that she'd be ready to go in with Sadie whenever she was ready.

Sadie noticed a couch sitting off to the side in the foyer and went to sit down. Straightening her shoulders, she took a deep breath and closed her eyes to pray for the first time in a long time. The triple shoulders + breath + prayer combination was one her grandmother had taught her to rely on whenever she was feeling nervous about what lay ahead.

'Sadie Campbell. There's hardly anything in this world that straight shoulders, a deep breath, and a talk with the Lord won't fix.'

And like most things, her grandmother had been right. She slowly leaned back and briefly closed her eyes.

'Ok God, you've brought me this far. Please help me get through the rest of the night.'

Opening her eyes and sitting up straighter, she looked around the foyer, fond memories from her childhood and youth flooding in. Looking around now she recalled running through the doors as a young girl with Scarlett by her side, their parents walking in behind them. She remembered running towards her Sunday School classroom and to the weekly Tuesday night Kids Club program, both girls excited to meet up with friends and share with their teacher the bible verse they had spent the week memorizing together.

It was in this church that Sadie had first attended youth group with her friends. She remembered Emily purposely seeking out where Jake was sitting the first night she had come, making sure they sat where he would see her. She recalled a couple of years later holding Mason's hand and squeezing it tightly as the youth pastor taught the teenagers about the importance of purity and saving your body for your husband or wife. She and Mason had shared those same values. Back then they had their whole life already planned out.

Turning now to look towards the parking lot, she could almost see her and her friends standing around the back of the church van, laughing and jamming bookbags, sleeping bags and pillows into the trunk- anticipation at its peak as they prepared to drive hours together to attend a youth rally out of town. Their youth leader ready for a steady rotation of Stephen Curtis Chapman, DC Talk and the Newsboys to be blaring through the speakers. She thought about that first road trip to a youth rally at another church, in another city, she had had a blast. She smiled as she remembered all-nighters that her own church had hosted. Leaders doing everything they could to help the kids stay awake, including 2AM pizza deliveries and 4AM water fights.

As a young adult she stood in the same foyer where she was sitting now, hearing soft music playing in the distance, studying her dad's face and holding tightly to his arm as they waited for the doors to the sanctuary to open so he could walk down her down the aisle through a gathering of family and friends, towards the man she was about to marry. *How had it gone so wrong?*

Shaking her head, she stood, took another deep breath, and made her way over to Emily. Emily, her best friend who stood in Sadie's kitchen three weeks ago and told Sadie how much she cared about her- how important she felt that it was that Sadie take this next step.

Sadie had seen that Emily had been nervous to ask her to come tonight and how important it had been to her. Emily wasn't the kind of friend who had just encouraged Sadie to come to talk to people she didn't know about this thing in her life that had been weighing on her so deeply; Emily hadn't given her a hug and sent her here with sentiments of thoughts and prayers... No, Emily was the kind of friend who was *here*, standing next to her, doing what she could to make sure her friend really was ok.

Sadie stood and made her way towards her closest friend.

"Ready?'" Emily asked as Sadie approached her.

"Yup, all good."

Sadie filled out her white stick-on nametag, attached it to her sweater over her chest, and began walking down the hall she knew so well, this time, towards the unknown.

Chapter Seven

Now

Turning into what used to be her old Sunday School classroom, Sadie first noticed how much cozier it felt tonight than any other time she'd seen the space. The room was lit only by lamps on corner tables and had couches and chairs set up in a circle in the middle of the room, spaced an arm's length apart from each other. To Sadie's left, a long white foldout table had been set up just inside the door. It was covered by a white tablecloth and was holding two trays of homemade cookies, an arrangement of fruits and vegetables, a serving tray of cubed cheese and crackers, a stainless-steel coffee carafe, a kettle that sat next to a wicker bowl filled with tea bags, mini containers of milk and cream, and a stack of paper cups and lids. Sadie was taken aback that someone had made that sort of an effort for this group of women. A smaller round table, also covered in a white table-cloth, sat next to the food table which held on it new bibles, DivorceCare pamphlets, cut outs of bible verses and an array of knitted scarves. The two friends noticed the scarves at the same time and while Sadie was thinking that they were probably left over from a group that met in this room before them, Emily walked over and started sorting through them, grabbing one and wrapping it loosely around her neck.

Emily saw Sadie's look of disbelief and replied, "What? They're lovely!"

"What if they're not for us to take?"

"What are you talking about? Why else would they be here?" Sometimes Emily just didn't understand Sadie's thought process.

Continuing around the room, the adjacent wall held a giant white board where someone had written in a mix of fall colors:

Welcome!

'The Lord is close to the brokenhearted and saves
those who are crushed in spirit.'
Psalms 34:18

Emily smiled, seeing the sign the same time Sadie did. She looked over at Sadie and nodded towards it, her eyebrows lifted towards her friend silently saying, *'See? That's what I told you too.'*

"Come on," Emily said then, "let's go find a seat."

They found an empty well-worn couch, one that looked like it had seen better days, and settled in next to each other. Sadie was fidgeting and trying to get comfortable. "I can't believe you took a scarf."

"What?" Emily smiled, "It's cute! You can never have too many homemade scarves!"

As a teenager, Sadie probably would have been placed in the 'tomboy' category by most. Emily though, had always loved spending her time and money on all things girly- hair accessories, makeup, clothes. She had spent her weekly allowance on magazines with thick glossy pages that were filled with perfume samples and runway models in designer clothing showcasing collections Emily knew she would never see in Darlings Lake. Emily had always been Sadie's most fashionable friend, and she highly doubted Emily currently owned any knitted scarves. The one Emily grabbed was made in deep rich colors- dark oranges, browns and burgundies in the softest yarn. It matched Emily's black jeans and black T-shirt, and complimented Emily's caramel complexion and dark hair perfectly.

With some women in the room still mingling and grabbing hot drinks, Sadie picked at a loose thread in her jeans and wondered what it was that she was supposed to say once the meeting started.

She had been curious on the drive over if she would know any of the women here tonight. Having grown up in Darlings, her experience had been that she ran into people she knew at most places that she went to. Whether it be the grocery store, the hardware store, or the gym, she was apt to run into someone she knew to exchange pleasantries with. On the way over she had resigned herself to the idea that she would likely be sitting here tonight with someone that she had gone to High School with, or a friend of a friend, someone who might make Sadie uncomfortable to freely share if asked to do so. Looking around, she was surprised to see that wasn't the case. There were women here of various ages, but no one other than Emily that she knew. *Huh.*

Promptly at 6:30 PM, the scheduled start time, an elderly lady sitting across from Sadie cleared her throat.

"Welcome, everyone" she began, "I'm so glad you could be here tonight. My name is Harriet. My friends call me Hattie, and I'm going to guide our discussion today."

Harriet was warm and softly spoken. She sat in an over-sized burgundy winged backed chair and Sadie thought she looked adorable in her pleated dress pants and cream-colored knitted sweater. Her grey hair was neatly styled in an updo that rested above the back of her neck. She held a bible loosely in her hands and looked to be about the same age as her Gram. The woman smiled as she spoke.

"This is week one of our group, so we're all beginning to-gether. You will notice that this *is* a group for women only. We prefer that those who attend are divorced." She stopped and chuckled to herself, "Well now, we don't want to see you divorced! We want the people in the group to be divorced... Oh dear, that's not what I meant either. Maybe I should start again." She continued, her cheeks a little pinker, "While this group is meant for those who have *been through* a divorce, it's also perfectly fine for us to bring a support person if anyone feels that they need it."

Sadie had never met Harriet before but she seemed to un-derstand the women here. "Just so you know what to expect, we'll begin by going around and sharing our name. After your name, you can share as much or as little as you'd like, keep-ing in mind there are about 10 of us here and one person shouldn't monopolize the evening. You might want to share why you feel like this group could be helpful for you or what you're hoping to get out of being here. If you are willing, you could also share how long you were married for, if you have children, or even how long you have been divorced for. Any information you share helps others to relate to you and understand a bit more of where you're coming from. You never know what you might share that could resonate with someone else. If you are here as a support person, you just need to say your name and who you are here to support."

"Before we get started," Harriet continued, "I'll just share for transparency's sake, that I have never been divorced." She placed her bible on the floor next to her and folded her hands in her lap. "I was married to a wonderful man for 52 years and as some of you know, he passed away just over two years ago." She paused, considering what she wanted to share, "Albie and I had been living in New Brunswick before he passed and one of our sons who lives here in Darlings, had a very tough time a few years ago when his marriage ended without warning. As I watched him try to navigate the healing process on his own and cope with all of his feelings, I kept praying that someone would come along and help him in a way that I knew Albie or I couldn't. He ended up agreeing to go to counselling and then joined a men's bible study here at this church, and both of those things made a world of difference for him. Then don't you know, when I was thanking God for his grace and mercy in my son's situation, he began placing on my heart women who were going through the same thing as my son. I tried to brush it off, really, I did. How could I be qualified to talk about divorce when I was so happy in my marriage? So, I promised God I would revisit his ask another time."

She lowered her voice a bit and said, "Isn't that so nice of me?"

The women chuckled.

"After Albie passed, I was quite lonely and was spending a lot of time talking on the phone to my boys, I have three. After much encouragement from them I decided to move back to Nova Scotia, we had only been over there for Albie's work. And as I was making plans to move, I was reminded of the promise I made to God, and I re-committed to seeing if there is some way I could help women going through difficult times. When I came back to this church, I connected with the pastor to see if there were any active ministries here specifically for women grieving or going through a divorce. When he said that no, there was not, I did what one does when they feel God pressing on their heart, I asked him about starting a group."

"Bless." Sadie heard Emily whisper.

Harriet continued, "Now, I'm not a counsellor and I don't have formal training to speak of, but I did join a support group for grief after my Albie passed, and I found it immensely helpful." Opening her bible, which Sadie could now see was tattered and well-used, a folded piece of paper lay between the pages. Pulling it out and opening the paper, Harriet looked around at the women in the circle and continued on. "I'm going to share with you the meeting etiquette guide that was shared with us during my grief support group, and I think it worked quite well. I've updated it a little because not everyone here tonight is grieving in the traditional sense of the word."

Harriet's tone was a perfect way to set the mood and intention for the evening and everyone was respectfully listening. Sadie's heart rate had started to slow.

"First off, everything that is shared here needs to stay here. This is important. Nobody wants to think that what they share here will be told to someone else who isn't here, or that their story, or some version of it, will be making its rounds in the community. We all know how unbecoming small-town gossip is."

"You're right." A girl sitting a few seats next to Sadie mumbled under her breath, she looked younger than Sadie, and more mad than sad.

"Secondly, let's lead with kindness. Just because someone's story is different from yours, or they are handling their situation in a way that you wouldn't, it doesn't make it any more right or wrong, or less impactful to the person. We are here mostly to listen, to give support where we can- not to share our opinions or thoughts on someone else's situation unless we're asked to do so." She paused, scanning her paper. "You know, there are others, but I think everything can fall into those two categories. Let's be kind and let's keep what we hear quiet. Oh, and please leave your cell phones in your bag or on silent. Each person here took time out of their evening to be here, so let's give that the attention and respect it deserves."

"Preach Hattie." Emily said as she nodded her approval. I guess she was on a friendship level with Harriet now.

"At my last group," Harriet leaned in as if she were telling the women a secret, "someone was sharing about their loss and what was on their heart, and the woman next to me took out her phone and started texting someone else! Can you imagine!? I was horrified... Gracious sake." Harriet shook her head and still looked bothered. "One last thing before we begin, we are gathered here in a church because I believe with everything in me that God helped me through my loss, and I have faith that he can help you too. I don't believe that any of us are here by chance, even me. Despite what some of you may believe in this moment, God loves each of us. Divorce is hard, but ladies, God doesn't shy away from hard, and... you are here, so you aren't shying away from it either." Sadie felt Emily nudge her. "Despite what we've each been through, he isn't finished with any of us just yet and if you hear nothing else tonight, please hear that despite having gone through what you have, you are still his daughter, and he still loves you."

Sadie wasn't expecting to get emotional tonight, but she could feel a deep pressure on her chest and her eyes well with tears. She looked up and tried to quickly blink them back.

Sadie's relationship with God had been touch-and-go for so long. There were times when she believed what Harriet had just shared, that obviously God loved her. When she looked in the faces of her children she would be overwhelmed with gratitude to Him, but that's not where she'd been camping out. More often than not, Sadie was angry with God- livid, actually. She knew in her life she'd made mistakes, but hadn't everyone? She had always tried to honour Him, had always tried to do the right thing, and really, where had it gotten her? She was divorced. She felt alone. Her kids were growing up in a home so different from what hers had been, and she couldn't think about it for too long lest she break down in tears, which she often did. She knew the 'right' things to do- 'be honest with God, tell Him how you feel', yada yada, but it hadn't worked. More often than not she wondered if God was even listening anymore. Where did he go? *Where did you go?*

It's now been years since things had gone so wrong, and she was still so tired, still feeling alone, still confused and still so guilty- so so guilty, all the time. Hearing Harriet say that God still loved her wasn't resonating with Sadie, at all.

Chapter Eight

Now

The night Emily had first asked Sadie to come to this meeting they had just gotten back from a long walk together. Emily was in Sadie's kitchen, getting herself a glass of water when she turned and looked at Sadie. "I need to talk to you."

Sadie had chuckled, "We just walked for an hour and talked the whole time!"

"I know," Emily had replied, "But the whole time we were walking and talking I was also praying, and I can't put this off any longer so, I'm just gonna say it."

"Ok. Go ahead." Sadie was worried but could also feel herself starting to get defensive even though she didn't know what was coming.

"I want you to come with me to a meeting at church next month. It's for divorced women and I think it could help you." She was staring at Sadie now and she looked none-too-pleased.

"Emily."

"I'm serious Sadie. I'm worried about you. I miss you."

"I see you all the time!"

"I know, I know, we see each other. I mean, I miss the Sadie that you used to be. The one who was always laughing and joking and calling me just to talk about camera angles and telephone lenses and all that stuff that I don't understand."

"Telephoto lenses."

"Yeah. Exactly. Whatever."

Sadie could see Emily was upset but felt that was unfair. Didn't she know that obviously Sadie would rather feel lighter than she did now? Who wanted to feel tired and angry and lost? Sadie had been trying to cover up how she was feeling but obviously wasn't doing a good enough job. Doesn't Emily know that she would do just about anything to feel like her old self again? So that's what she told her.

"That's my point Sadie!" Emily had responded. "Here is something I think you can do. Come to this meeting with me! I'll come with you, so you don't have to go alone. There's an older lady that's going to be leading it, and when I heard her talking about it at church, I kept thinking of you."

Sadie pushed back again but Emily had a response for each objection. Now, contemplating the suggestion, she was feeling a weird mixture of indignation and hope. *Could it help?* Even though the meeting was in a church and she had been questioning almost every day why God had turned his back on her, she wondered if maybe this would be the thing that could help her start to move forward.

Sadie was a smart and educated woman, and when she was honest with herself, she knew what Emily had just said was right. She had been feeling off, and of course others could feel it too. Sadie wanted to move forward. She felt like her life had been picked up and rearranged into a riddle that she never asked for, one she couldn't figure out how to solve. The worst part was that she knew deep down that her heart wouldn't settle until she did. What often made it worse, when she let herself go there, was that she remembered times when she was genuinely and purely happy- when she felt care-free and had a plan of where her life would lead. Sadie still thrived on plans, but for the last few years she couldn't imagine feeling as motivated and excited about life as she had been then.

A few years after Sadie had been married, she had taken a Sunday afternoon boat ride with some friends and had captured a picture of a weathered buoy floating in the ocean. She had been struck at the idea of this small object left bobbing alone in such a vast sea, silently and faithfully serving a purpose to those who came across it. She loved that picture- the idea of being needed but also alone had resonated with her, even then. She had titled the photograph 'Sentry at Sea', and when showing it to a client, they had suggested that she enter it in the Nature Canada Photo Contest. She did and it had gone on to take the first-place prize.

Her eyebrows were furrowed. She didn't want to feel like a buoy any longer.

"So will you come?" Emily interrupted her thoughts, "Please?"

And now, as she sat listening to Harriet talk about God, Sadie knew exactly why she felt so heavy.

There were people who could easily reconcile that divorce happened. Some skeptics she knew viewed it as inevitable from the outset- people grew apart, they changed what they wanted, behaviors that were once condoned became exasperated once married, new behaviors began, or worse, were discovered. People could justify divorce all they wanted, but Sadie knew better. She had grown up in church. She had listened to pastors in all stages of her life preach about how marriage is God's gift and how divorce is a sin.

In its nature, true love is designed to persevere, so the bible says, but Sadie's love didn't, if it was even real love in the first place. Sadie wasn't always sure. And her marriage, well, it didn't feel like a gift, and the bible doesn't really talk about that now does it? What she *does* know is that she disappointed herself. She let down her kids, her parents, Scarlett and Emily. They've never said that of course, or even made her to feel like she's disappointed them but she feels it regardless, deep in her bones in fact, and to come and hear in a group that Sadie was still God's daughter and that he loved her, well, it felt like salt in a wound. Because she hadn't loved God enough to stay in her marriage.

Maybe she just wasn't ready for this type of meeting like she thought she was. How was she going to make progress or be all-in if she couldn't even get behind the message of night one? Looking around the room at the other women who had begun to introduce themselves, Sadie felt disappointment wash over her. She had hoped this would help. And despite Harriet's last comments, Sadie really liked her and felt that her intentions here tonight were genuine.

She reminded herself that she had promised Emily that she would give it a real shot, and she would keep her promise to her best friend. She was too in her head, she knew, and she didn't know how she was going to sit here for the rest of the meeting and pretend otherwise.

Chapter Nine

Then

Sadie woke up on her 15th birthday on the bottom bunk of a bed that she shared with her good friend and fellow camp counsellor, Rachel.

Unlike Sadie, Rachel wasn't from Darlings Lake. Her family lived a couple of hours away in Chester, but her parents, who had grown up in the Darlings area, had been sending her to Camp Hope ever since she'd been old enough to come. Sadie and Rachel met the first time either of them had ever attended an overnight camp. They were both going into grade two and had been assigned to stay in the same cabin.

Sadie had been sitting cross-legged on her sleeping bag putting together a friendship bracelet for Emily, waiting for other kids to arrive and feeling a little homesick, when she heard a loud BANG reverberate through the cabin. Sadie looked up in shock and saw that a girl that she didn't know had just walked straight into the closed screen door of the cabin. The inside cabin door was open, but the outside screen door had always stayed shut to keep out the bugs.

This girl with two long red braided pigtails had been holding an open box of chocolate milk and the chocolate milk was now all over the front of her new camp t-shirt. Sadie's eyes were wide as she sat frozen in shock and tried not to stare. The little girl threw her box on the ground and flew open the screen door. Standing in the doorway with her hands on her hips she looked around the cabin and saw Sadie sitting there stunned, staring back at her.

"Did you see that?" the girl asked.

"Um... Yeah." Sadie tentatively replied.

"Well, I did that on purpose."

"Oh... yeah?"

"Yep. I like chocolate milk so much I wanted to wear it!"

Sadie noticed then that the girl was smiling.   With that, Sadie burst into giggles and fell to her side. "Are you ok?" She said when she had finally stopped laughing.

"Yeah, what a dumb door! I'm Rachel. What's your name?"

"Sadie"

"Ok Lady Sadie, can you help me with my stuff?"

With that, Sadie hopped off the lower bunk bed and started helping Rachel drag in her sleeping bag, pillow, blanket, stuffy and duffle bag. Rachel preferred the top bunk so naturally she chose the bed above Sadie.

When Rachel's mom walked in and saw the two girls talking together she smiled, happy that Rachel had already met someone, and then noticing her daughter's shirt exclaimed, "Rachel, what in the world!?"

"Sorry mom, it jumped out of the box." Rachel shrugged and kept unpacking, grinning at Sadie. Sadie smiled back and crawled up to the top bunk where Rachel would be sleeping, helping her arrange everything the way she thought she would want it. She couldn't believe how cool Rachel was. If that would have just happened to her, she would've cried for sure.

Sadie had wanted Emily to come to camp with her that summer, but last month she'd learned that every summer, as soon as school ended, Emily's mom took her to Mexico for almost the whole summer to visit with her abuelos. Her dad would join them for a week or two, but Emily's mom told Sadie's mom that she and Emily would usually be gone all of July and most of August.

It was only the middle of July and Sadie was already missing Emily like crazy, but with this new girl here now, Sadie thought that maybe it would be ok. And as it turned out it was- Sadie and Rachel had spent that first week by each other's side and couldn't wait for the next week they'd get to spend together.

There had only been one summer in the last nine that Rachel didn't come to Camp Hope the same week as Sadie. The year following the summer that they missed, the girls decided that if they could help it, they wouldn't miss another. They exchanged home addresses and from that summer on, committed to being pen pals. They sent each other handwritten letters through the year, keeping up on each other's lives, and as the time for camp registration grew near, they confirmed the weeks they'd attend so they would be sure to be there together. As Sadie got older, writing to Rachel was added to her monthly schedule and it was a time that she looked forward to. She had a special box at the top of her closet for notes that friends gave her in school, ones that she wanted to keep, and she put the letters she received from Rachel in there as well.

The year before this one, both girls had decided to apply to work at Camp Hope and after going through the interview process, were thrilled to have both been offered a position. Each had immediately asked the Managing Director if the other had been hired as well.

They were now junior counsellors and shared a bunkbed in a room that felt like the size of a closet. Their room was attached to, but also separated from, the main room where the campers slept. They were close enough to the campers that they could hear a camper if she woke, but far enough away that they could talk after lights out without waking the kids. The two senior counsellors were in a bunk bed right next to them. The four teenagers had never had less personal space, nor had they ever loved a room more.

"Morning birthday girl!" Rachel jumped down off the top bunk and threw herself onto Sadie who was still half asleep, wrapping her arms around her sleepy friend as well as the blankets, pillow and stuffed bear she slept with each night.

"Rachel!" Sadie was smothered in Rachel's body weight but couldn't help the smile that peaked out.

"Big day!" Rachel talked into the blanket covering Sadie's head, so it all came out muffled. "I love you so much."

"I love *you* so much," Sadie replied, out of breath and trying to push Rachel off her, "But Gosh girl, you need to lay off the chocolate milk. You're... heavy."

"Sadie Campbell! You brat!" With that, Rachel started to shake her and then sprung up, banging her head on the base of the top bunk. She rolled over and grabbed her head "Ow!"

Sadie laughed and sat up. After she made sure her friend was ok, the two got ready for the day.

Days at camp were like clockwork because they operated on a strict schedule. Campers arrived on Sunday afternoons and then for the most part, Mondays looked like Tuesdays, Tuesdays looked like Wednesdays and Thursdays. Campers left on Friday after lunch and the staff spent the afternoon cleaning. When all the cabins, washrooms and shared buildings were clean and ready for the following week, the kitchen staff made pizza and everyone ate together, exhausted but happy. It was the summer camp grind, and you had to be built for it. Some staff stayed into Friday evening to hang out with each other without the campers around. They'd eat, have a campfire, and share funny stories from the week. The kids were awesome, but Friday nights were the highlight of Sadie's summer. She usually only ever got home around midnight and then would sleep most of Saturday before starting it all again on Sunday. This year, as luck would have it, Sadie's 15th birthday fell on a Friday.

The campers had left hours earlier and the staff had received the all-clear that cleanup was over. She and Rachel were now in their cabin getting ready for supper, taking longer getting ready tonight than they normally did. Sadie had loosely curled her shoulder-length brown hair, adding some bounce to it, and put on a light layer of makeup, including for the first time, the new mascara that Emily had gifted her before she left for the summer. It was her birthday after all, and she had asked her parents if it would be ok if she could stay at camp for the evening and then celebrate her birthday with them tomorrow. She had heard the initial disappointment in her mom's voice when she had asked earlier in the week, but her mom had rebounded quickly and said that yes, of course, if that's what she wanted then no problem. Sadie was thankful and looked forward to seeing her mom when she picked her up tonight at 11, but first, she was looking forward to a night with her camp friends and wanted to feel pretty on her birthday.

"Any big plans for your birthday night?" Rachel asked, glancing at her through the mirror she was using to straighten her long red hair, "with... Mason maybe?"

Sadie blushed and looked over at Rachel. They were alone so they could talk freely.

"No... why would you ask that?"

"I don't know, you talk about him all the time in your letters, but you don't really hang out with him when you're both here, not that I can see anyway. I just didn't know if you had a thing for him. Sadie, he's hot. Super-hot. If you want to go get it, you totally should."

"I'm not *going to get it* Rach. That's weird. It's Mason." Sadie replied, and unconsciously slid the back of her hand up to feel her cheek, which had suddenly looked extra pink.

"Ok great," Rachel paused, then turned to face Sadie. "I have something to ask you then."

"K, Shoot."

"If you're *for sure* not interested," Rachel continued slowly, "I was thinking maybe, I could ask Mason out?"

"What?" Sadie turned to Rachel, "Are you serious?"

"Well," Rachel responded, "I mean yeah, if you're not going to. I know it would be tough to date through the school year, but I think we could make it work. We get along really well, he's funny, and well- so hot."

Sadie was truly baffled, the idea catching her totally off guard. She didn't know what to say. She didn't want to tell Rachel no, but this was Mason. *Her* Mason. She didn't talk to him a lot at camp because they were with different groups of kids and assigned to different activities. She was on swimming duty helping the lifeguard down by the lake, and he was up in the field helping kids with archery and scavenger hunts. They just weren't around each other that much, but she did know when he was around- she could feel it. And what was Rachel talking about? They always talked. And yeah, of course she knew how good looking he was. His looks had totally changed this past year. He had gone from tall and kind of scrawny to more... filled out.

He had asked her last year at a Christmas dinner his family was hosting if in January she might want to go to the gym with him on the mornings before school when he didn't have hockey practice. It was nice that he asked but she had ultimately said no- she had no interest in getting up earlier than she already had to for school, and besides, she had a long-standing after-school gym routine with Emily. But seeing him this summer in shorts and T-shirts? She could see he was going without her. He had actual defined muscles now. Why *wouldn't* Rachel be interested in him, she thought suddenly. She didn't like it, but she wasn't ready to say that out loud yet either.

"Sure Rachel, I mean, if you like him then yeah, you should totally ask him to do something with you sometime." She looked away and started to put in her earrings.

"Sadie." Rachel said.

Sadie ignored her, trying to think of something else.

"Sadie!" Rachel said louder.

"What!?" Sadie turned and snapped.

Rachel came over then and stood behind Sadie, both images reflecting back at them in Sadie's mirror. Rachel slowly turned Sadie around so that they were face to face. "Sadie, I don't like Mason. I'm not going to ask him out." She grabbed her friend's shoulders and smiled, "But, I know that YOU do. I see how you two look at each other."

"You're mean." Sadie looked up at her friend then, who was a few inches taller than her.

Rachel chuckled. "I'm not mean. I'm trying to *help* you. You've been talking about him for years Sade, and this summer I'm definitely noticing how much he's watching you when you aren't looking at him."

"Really?"

"Yes, really. And because he's so good looking, and so freaking nice, and such a good hockey player, some other girl *is* going to want to go out with him. I'm sure they do already. When we were all cleaning the bathrooms this afternoon, I heard Carrie and Jessica talking about the guys at camp and they spent a lot of time talking about Mase." She gave Sadie the *'you know what I'm talking about'* look. "I just wouldn't want you guys to get into this weird friend zone because you've known each other for so long and miss something that's right in front of you. Look at you! You're beautiful. You're young, it's your birthday! Enjoy your night! Go get that first kiss!"

"Rachel, no."

"Yes! Why not? I'm telling you. That feeling you felt when you thought I might like him? That feeling is going to come around for real one day and it won't be me pretending. I'm just saying."

"Ok, message received. Can we go now?"

"Sure, Lady Sadie. It's your special day. I'll leave it. Besides, I heard your mom might have dropped off a cake for all of the staff to help you celebrate your birthday."

"What? She did not."

"She did. Because she loves you. And so do I. And.... maybe so does... Mason?"

"Enough!" But Sadie was smiling. She took one final look in the mirror and a deep breath, "Ok, lets go."

Chapter Ten

Then

All through supper Sadie couldn't shake what Rachel had said but tried her best to push it aside. And after supper, when the Camp Director brought out the cake her mom had delivered and everyone sang happy birthday to her, she had zoned out in the middle of it. Multiple times through the evening she even had to ask people to repeat themselves. She just couldn't stay focused.

Sitting in the lodge and thinking about it now, Rachel was right, Sadie knew, even if she hadn't been ready to admit it. But this was Mason Gray, she couldn't be more than friends with him... could she? What would their parents think? They'd known each other their whole lives. What if she told him how she might be feeling and it ruined everything? If he wasn't interested in her like that, and she told him she was, he could end their friendship- never talk to her again. That would be horrible. No, she was better off not saying anything and staying friends with him. She wouldn't risk giving up what they had now- an easiness that she didn't have with any other guys. It was something she didn't take for granted. So what if Mason started dating someone else? It was bound to happen. She would still be his friend, and they could just all hang out together. Couldn't they? She was sure her and Mason would just talk about his girlfriend when she wasn't around; like they talked about everything else. They could still walk the path between their homes and sit and watch the frogs after it rained... right? Or, once he got a girlfriend would he not have time for her anymore? That would suck. But not as much as it would suck if she told him she might like him and he laughed at her, that would be way worse. No, she didn't want to take a chance and risk embarrassing herself. But she also didn't think she wanted him to date anyone else. She was in a serious catch 22. She could feel her brows deeply furrowed and quickly tried to relax her face, looking around to see if anyone had noticed. Thankfully, everyone seemed to be engaged in their own conversations.

She scanned the room to find Rachel, who was leaned in and engrossed in a story Carrie was telling her about one of their campers. The guys sat at the long table behind Rachel and Carrie. Mason was leaning back in a chair with his hat on backwards, his brown hair flipped out under the sides. This year he had grown his hair out longer and she loved it. She had even told him so when she noticed it this Spring.

Mason was listening to Matt now, one of the other guys at the table- who was using his whole body to tell a story, and she was watching as he began laughing. The laughter at the table got louder and she saw Mason raise his hand and tell his buddy to 'please stop' while wiping tears from his eyes. Sadie found herself chuckling watching them have so much fun.

Mason looked over at Sadie just then, and still smiling, gave her a quick wink. It was so fast, Sadie wondered if she had imagined it, but felt her stomach physically flip over, so thought it must have actually happened. She quickly looked behind her to see if that wink was meant for someone else. When she saw no one standing there, she turned back and saw Mason still smiling in her direction, this time giving her an almost imperceptible nod of the head.

Just then they all heard someone announce that the campfire by the lake was 'epic' and anyone that wanted to, should make their way down to where the firepit was. Sadie looked over at Rachel and they both stood up to head down together, making a quick stop at their cabin first to pick up sweaters.

Walking in the dark toward their cabin, Sadie was contemplating the whole night- from Rachel's comments to her own worries, and lastly to how her body was still reacting to Mason's wink. Without thinking about it for too long, Sadie reached into the bottom of her overnight bag and pulled out Mason's white sweater, the one she had taken from his room last month. She hadn't ever worn it after that evening, and Mason had never asked for it back. She wasn't sure if he even realized she still had it. She had intended to give it back to him while they were here but had forgotten. She threw it on now over her tank top and jean shorts, quickly changing her sandals into sneakers. Rachel hadn't seen Mason wear the sweater through the school year, so didn't register Sadie's silent gambit.

Sadie and Rachel arrived at the campfire after a few others were already there. They sat a few spaces away from each other on one of the wooden benches, but close enough that they could still hear the other. With the campers gone, it was nice to have the time and space around the campfire to themselves. The wood hissed and crackled on the ground within the hand-made circular stone wall. The rocks underneath creating a pedestal for the flames that danced across the burning logs. The glow from the fire provided the only source of light for those sitting nearby.

A neat pile of wood had been stacked near the firepit, the light from the campfire highlighting the work someone had gone through to ensure that the fire could easily be tended to as needed.

Sadie looked to the sky and noticed the stars had also begun to make an appearance. Naturally as breathing, she thanked God for the fire, for such a beautiful night, and for letting her spend her birthday and her summer, at camp. She loved it here so much and sometimes felt bad for the kids who didn't get to experience this, even though they didn't know what they were missing.

She could hear the voices of the group of guys getting louder as they made their way down from the main lodge towards the campfire. Matt had already started singing, loud and off-pitch, and she could see in the distance that he had brought his guitar with him. Watching the shadows and voices turn into clearer versions of her friends and fellow counsellors, her heart rate started to pick up slightly. She was nervous to see Mason's reaction when he saw her sitting there in his sweater.

As the guys approached the benches and began looking for seats, they did the same thing her and Rachel had- sitting next to each other but a few spaces apart. She saw Mason then, at the back of the group. He was wearing a heavy black hoodie and had flipped his hat around so that the bill sat low on his forehead. He looked as relaxed and as handsome as she'd ever seen him.

Mason stopped at the end of the path and scanned the benches, trying to decide where he wanted to sit when his eyes fell on Sadie. His breath caught as he saw her, instantly recognizing the sweater she was wearing. She was watching him and he stood still and tried to regulate his breath. She gave him a small tentative wave, and he realized he was probably staring, but he couldn't take his eyes off her. She no longer looked like the little Sadie Campbell that he had grown up with- his neighbor and childhood best friend, the girl he'd spent hours with, without glancing twice at. No, tonight he couldn't help but look at her. His body was betraying him and wouldn't let him look away. Long earrings peaked through her curled hair, which brushed the neckline of his old worn sweater, and he noticed she had tucked the end of his sweater into her jean shorts. Faded sneakers and firm tan legs completed the rest of her silhouette. Mason couldn't believe how much older she looked tonight, beautiful even. He didn't have to think twice, he knew where he'd be sitting.

Sadie saw Mason pause and stare at her under his ball hat, a confused look on his face. She gave him a little wave, but he didn't respond or acknowledge her at all. God, she hoped he wasn't upset with her. *What had she been thinking!?*

One of the younger guys sitting a few benches over from Sadie yelled, "Hey Mase! Over here!"

But Mason shook his head, "Nah man, I'm good." And he made his way over to where Sadie was sitting.

She looked up at him as he stood in front of her, his hands in his pockets. He nodded to the open spot directly to her right, "May I?"

"Yeah," she stuttered, "yeah, of course."

She glanced over at Rachel who was smiling at her. She gave Sadie a subtle thumbs up and turned back to watch the flames.

Mason lowered himself on the bench next to her. He was sitting close enough that she could feel his jeans against her bare leg. He nudged her with his leg and leaned over, resting his elbows on his knees. They sat quietly for a moment before he looked over at her. "I like that sweater."

She caught his grin through the light of the fire. "Yeah, me too."

"It looks better on you." He wasn't smiling anymore.

She smiled looking ahead and nudged him with her shoulder. "Aww."

Matt pulled out his guitar then and began taking requests from the group. Together the teens sang hits from Third Eye Blind, the Backstreet Boys and Notorious B.I.G, laughing as a group as Matt attempted to rap, failing miserably. They then moved into Christian classics like 'Shine Jesus Shine' and 'Awesome God', after the final verse of 'I love You Lord' the group was quiet and pensive, each appreciating the quiet after a long week.

After a few minutes of quiet, Matt started to strum his guitar again slowly and began singing "Happy Birthday to you...," the group collectively smiled and they all joined in, "Happy Birthday to you, Happy Birthday Lady Sadie...Happy birthday to you." Sadie laughed and bowed from where she was sitting, thanking them for the song. Matt put his guitar away and everyone began talking, back to connecting with their friends. One by one people started to get up and leave, walking up the hill towards the main lodge, where staff vehicles and parents who were on pick-up duty sat waiting.

Rachel came over and leaned down, whispering to Sadie, "Have a good night, Sade. I'm headed up to bed." Standing, she added with a grin, "We'll catch up on Sunday." Giving Mason a quick smile and nod, she turned to walk back up the path. Because Rachel lived so far away, she stayed at the camp through the weekends. She loved having the place pretty much to herself and had only occasionally taken Sadie up on her offer to come home with her on the weekends.

Sadie looked at her watch and knew she still had another half an hour before her mom would be here. It was only her and Mason left, aside from one other couple on the opposite side of the fire. She watched the guy as he picked up what was left of the pile of wood and add it to the fire. He took his girlfriend's hand, and they headed up the path together.

"Mason," he turned then and said, "There's a couple buckets of water behind this bench for when you're done."

Mason nodded at him, acknowledging the unspoken direction.

Now Sadie sat next to Mason, the last two remaining by the fire. Sadie's stomach flipped again thinking about Mason's wink from earlier, and she wiped her hands on the sleeves of the sweater, feeling them warm and starting to sweat. She didn't know how tonight was going to end, but she knew that either way, by the end of it she would know where she and Mason stood.

She took a deep breath and mirroring the posture he'd resumed after the other couple left, she leaned in and placed her elbows on her knees. "So," she said after enough time had passed with neither of them speaking that she felt she had to be the one to break the silence.

"So," he said, turning to look at her. His eyes were such a light brown that sometimes they looked blue. She was noticing them now, under his hat, when he sat back up straighter and looked down at her. Watching her, he lowered his arm to his side, slowly turning his wrist and opening the palm of his left hand wide, resting it on the bench next to Sadie. His thumb brushed the side of her leg, just above her knee.

Surprised by his touch, she looked down at his hand and then slowly up to his face, her heart starting to pound faster than it ever had before. She sat up and was staring down at his hand, her mind racing and wondering if his intention was what she thought it was. She looked over at Mason again.

Watching her, his hand still open, he gave her a gentle nod.

She took her right hand and laid it in his. Her fingers were much smaller than his and she moved her hand up so that she could link her fingers through his. As soon as she folded them in around his, Mason closed his hand, lightly squeezing hers to keep it shut. He turned his wrist back towards himself so that they looked like any other couple sitting next to the fire, holding hands.

She knew she had to say something, but for the life of her couldn't think of what it should be. Mason had taken the lead and in his typically quiet fashion, was able to show her that he had been feeling the same way she was. Mason Gray was holding her hand and she loved it and her heart was racing and she was scared to say anything that would ruin the moment. Time was also passing and she didn't want to make it weird.

"You don't need to make this weird." Mason suddenly said, grinning at her.

"I'm not!" She laughed but quickly glanced again at their hands. She had never held anyone's hand before and was surprised how the warmth and tightness of his hand felt like it was meant to cover hers. She didn't want to let go.

He turned to her then, still holding her hand and used his other hand to pull his hat up a bit.

"I didn't want to ruin anything," he said.

"I didn't either."

He nodded. "I like you Sade."

"Yeah, I like you too."

"Like, a lot."

"Me too." She felt him squeeze her hand again, the crackling of the fire the only background sound.

"I didn't want to tell you." He continued on, "I was nervous you'd be like, 'dude, no'."

She laughed again, "Is that what I sound like?"

He smiled, "No, I guess not. I just don't want anything to change." He looked down at their hands then and added, "Well, maybe a few things."

She blushed. "When did you realize you liked me?"

"After school ended I think. I've just been thinking of you all the time, and watching you take pictures this summer- when we were on that path, you looked so happy, like you were truly in your element... and you were wearing my sweater," he pulled on her sleeve, "this sweater... and I realized how cool you actually are."

She smiled. "Actually cool."

He chuckled then, "You're right, you've always been cool... pretty, maybe I mean?"

She looked at him, not wanting to say anything to ruin how she was feeling.

"And then we got here this summer, and you were doing your own thing, and sometimes I could hear you laugh across the room or whatever, and I started wondering who was making you laugh, because I wanted to be the guy that made you laugh."

Sadie's heart was pounding. "That's really sweet," Sadie said, meaning it.

"And then when I saw you looking at me tonight..."

"You WINKED at me!"

Mason chuckled, "Did it work?"

"What? The wink?"

"Yeah," He looked sheepishly at Sadie, "My dad told me that the quickest way to let a girl know that you like her is to wink at her." He laughed then, "He said, 'Mason, don't wink at just anybody, because once they get a taste of the Gray charm, they'll be done for'."

Sadie laughed out loud. "Well, it worked."

"I'm glad," he said, turning serious again, "I want to date you Sadie. I want to be your boyfriend, and I want you to be my girlfriend. I want to be able to hold your hand whenever I want," he turned to her and brought his other hand to the ends of her hair, pulling it on it slightly, "...and kiss you when I want, and know that if someone else does make you laugh, that I'll get to hear about it later."

"I'd like that."

"Yeah?"

Saddie nodded, "Yeah."

"Awesome." Moving in closer to her, he let go of her hand and instead wrapped it around Sadie's back, gently pulling her in closer to him. He lifted his hat and drew closer to her, stopping to look at her eyes, checking to see that she was ok. When it felt like she was he whispered, "Happy Birthday Sadie," then slowly leaned in until his lips touched hers. Her lips, softer than he had even imagined, gently pressed back in return, letting him know that this was ok and that it was what she wanted too.

Sadie's heart was exploding and when Mason pulled back from her, he smiled. She went to find his hand to hold again and rested her head on his shoulder as they watched the flames. She couldn't imagine that any birthday would ever be better than this one.

Chapter Eleven

Now

Sadie jogged through the church parking lot, tightly gripping an umbrella that was doing what it could to protect her from the downpour. Darlings' weather- the sun was shining one minute, and it was pouring down rain the next. She had always found the sudden change in weather amusing, like God was trying to pull a fast one on them. Tonight though, the rain was coming down hard enough that she probably could have found a way to use it as an excuse not to leave her home. But while it had still been sunny, she had texted Emily and assured her that she still planned to go to DivorceCare that evening, adding that she was ok to go by herself and didn't need Emily to come with her. Once Emily was certain that Sadie was serious, she relinquished the pushback and told her that she'd only be a call or text away if she needed anything.

Walking now into the same low-lit room in the church, Sadie grabbed a cookie and made herself a cup of tea, moving to sit on the same couch that she had sat on with Emily the week before. She realized as she sat down that coming this second week had been easier than the first. She knew what to expect, and through her day had even looked forward to seeing Harriet and the other women here tonight. She stuck to wearing her jeans and sneakers, but this week she replaced her hoodie with a long sleeved pink cashmere sweater. She was warm and comfortable, and had taken note last week that everyone else, aside from Harriet, had dressed just as casually.

As people settled in their seats, Sadie noticed that this week there were small packages of tissue paper available by some of the chairs. Last week a couple of the women had become quite emotional sharing their stories and someone had had to leave to get some Kleenex. *So thoughtful*, Sadie thought looking around, that someone had been paying so much attention to the needs of the women.

Sadie hadn't needed tissue paper last week, because when introductions had made their way around to her, she had been polite and engaged, but brief in her statement, compared to others.

"Hi everyone," Sadie had begun, "My name is Sadie and I've lived here in Darlings all of my life, except for a few years when I went away to school. I got married after university, when I was 21, too young I think... it was for me anyway. My marriage started off ok, and then, well, then it wasn't ok. I learned quickly that we had different expectations of what marriage should be, how we should treat each other, and if I'm being completely honest, since I've had some time to think about it, and when I'm being really honest with myself, I feel like I pressured him into getting married in the first place. I really wanted to, I thought it was what God wanted for us, but I don't think he was ready for that kind of commitment. He told me once in a fight that he had never wanted to get married to begin with."

Sadie had taken a deep breath then, her eyes filled with tears, but she blinked them back, glancing up to see a few of the women nodding silently while others were looking at her with pity. Emily had reached for her hand, "That feeling you feel in your chest when someone you love says that to you... it summarizes the feeling I felt most often when I was married. Hurt and heavy, really confused. I cried a lot. I knew he wasn't happy, but I couldn't figure out why." She paused, "And now, well as Emily can attest," she looked at her friend, then back to the group, "I guess I've gone between mad and sad for the last five years since he left. Mostly mad at God. How come I did something that I thought he wanted for me, and I ended up so... sad? And then I look at my kids, I have 10-year-old twins, Tess and Jacob, and then I remember I have so much to be thankful for. I just forget that sometimes." Then with a shrug, nodded at Harriet indicating she was done talking for now. Harriet had thanked her for sharing, then smiled and nodded to the woman sitting next to her, letting her know it was now her turn.

It had felt good to say out loud what she had been keeping bottled up. Inherently she knew it was a step in the right direction, but it hadn't felt yet like she was any closer to closure. Still, she was curious about how she'd be feeling at the end of the five weeks, once she'd attended all of the meetings.

"Welcome back everyone!" Harriet began tonight. "I very much enjoyed getting to know each of you a little bit last week and we have a new friend joining us tonight. This is

Diya," Harriet gestured to her right. "Diya and I spoke earlier this evening, and she is aware of the group etiquette. Diya, thank you for coming! Would you like to introduce yourself and share with the group this evening?"

"Sure." Diya nodded.

She was young. Sadie couldn't imagine that she had been old enough to be married, let alone divorced, but then again, Sadie had only been 21 when she had made her vows.

"I'm Diya. My friends call me Dee." she began, looking at Harriet who nodded for her to continue.

"I'm 23. My husband, er... ex-husband Avi, he and I, we only got married two years ago." Her chin started to quiver, she looked down, took a moment and then looked back up, staring at no one in particular. "We don't have any kids. We both wanted to have kids. We talked about it all the time and it was one of the reasons that we got married so young and so early into our relationship, so that we could start our family together. I have seven siblings, and he has eight... big families are all we've known, and... all we wanted." She paused, taking a deep breath and reached for the tissue paper someone had leaned over to hand her. "About six months into our marriage, some really serious health issues that I'd been having for a while sort of came to a head. I won't get into all of that here because it's a different story for a different day, and actually probably requires a different type of support group, but, when all was said and done, when I left the hospital, I was no longer able to have children."

Sadie felt like she had been punched in the stomach, and soft gasps echoed around the room.

"Avi just... couldn't handle it. He's a good man, really, he is, but no matter how many options we looked at to begin to start having a family, he felt *so* strongly that he needed to have his own children- naturally, and only with his wife. And, well, since I could no longer have children, that... was it. I got home from the hospital and when I started to get my strength back and started to feel like myself again- he told me that he needed some space."

"Oh no..." An older lady sitting across the room whispered.

"Yeah. It's really hard." Diya went on. "I know in my head that my sickness wasn't my fault or in my control, but I don't know why of anything that I could have been diagnosed with, it had to be this. I mean, knowing how much we wanted kids...and God wants all marriages to work, you know? I would have tried to make it work. I did try. I came up with options. I wanted kids. As much as he did." Her words were coming out fast and she sounded like she just wanted to finish so she could get it over with.

"You can still have kids Diya." Another lady offered gently.

"Yeah, and someday I know I will. I mean, I really hope I will. But I'm 23 and divorced now and who wants that? Certainly no one in India, where I'm from- and want to go back to soon. For right now I'm just trying to get through each day and sort through all these feelings- anger, frustration, disappointment, so much sadness. I feel stressed all the time. I cried for months after he told me he couldn't stay. He cried too, just telling me. He said he was too young to... and I quote, 'settle'."

"Dang. So much for sickness and health." The woman next to me murmured.

"Yeah, that's what I said." Diya responded, hearing her. "We decided to take some time and separate, so he could work through his feelings, but once he moved out, that was it. The beginning of the end. There was a knock on our apartment door one day and when I opened it no one was there. I looked down and there laying on my doormat was a big yellow envelope. Divorce papers." She wiped at her eyes, "And what was I going to do? Not sign them and make him stay married to me knowing how much he wanted his own children?" Tears were sliding down her cheeks. "No. I signed the stupid papers and returned them to the envelope that was addressed to his lawyer- postage already pre-paid," she let out a half smile, "how kind. I received the fully signed and stamped papers back, confirming it was all over, just a few months ago now."

Sadie wanted to cross the room and hug her; what she was sharing was devastating. Diya took a deep breath and continued, "I started coming to this church with a friend about six months ago, and when I saw that there was this group coming up, I thought that I probably needed to be here. I couldn't make myself come last week."

"What you've shared is a lot for someone to have gone through Diya." Harriet responded. "Not just the divorce, but a medical situation as well."

She nodded at Harriet and smirked like, *'you're telling me'*. "When Avi and I met and had such similar backgrounds, it felt like fate." She shook her head and continued, "Physically, I'm feeling a lot better and the doctors remain positive. My family is back in India and not having them here has actually probably helped me more than hurt me. They have *lots* of opinions," Diya smiled. "They are still so mad at Avi, and when we facetime and I see them so hurt for me... and really, while the support is nice their hurt just adds to mine, like I brought this onto them. And yeah, I know- I'm working through that- just taking it one day at a time."

Hearing Diya talk about having divorce papers delivered to her door brought Sadie back to her experience with receiving her own. On a snowy winter day, her parents had come to visit her and the kids and had stopped at the mailbox at the end of her driveway, picking up her mail so Sadie wouldn't have to make the trek down the driveway to retrieve it. After initial greetings, they had left all the mail on the kitchen counter and had continued with their visit. That evening when everyone had gone and Sadie was cleaning up, she pulled out of the pile a manilla envelope stamped with an Ontario lawyer's address on it. She had crumbled. She knew what it held. Signing the paperwork at the same kitchen table that their family had celebrated so many different occasions had felt like the worst form of cruelty. She had donated that kitchen table and bought a new one the very next day.

And that's how the support group continued. One woman after another added to the story they had shared the week before. Some of the women had children, some didn't. Some had initiated their divorces themselves and others had it thrust upon them, like Diya. Each processing their own situation and working through feelings of confusion, guilt, anger, sadness... heartbreak. One woman without children was feeling guilty because of how happy she had been since her divorce and was worried she was turning into a walking poster child for it. Some women were working with a counsellor, others weren't.

The theme of the night was on coping mechanisms, and Sadie thought some of the suggestions would probably be helpful. She was already physically active, but she hadn't picked up her journal in a long time and thought that could be something that she could start doing again. Getting all of her thoughts out of her head so she could begin to try and maybe organize and work through them. Sadie also knew she had to talk to a counsellor and considered how she could go about making an appointment. She figured that if she really was going to face her situation head on, to try and move forward, she might as well really go for it.

There had been less talk of God this week and by the end of the meeting, Sadie realized that Emily had been right-this was good for her. She had even caught herself laughing, twice. She was always amazed how some people have a natural ability to look on the positive side of a circumstance despite how they feel, and she had been encouraged to realize that when she had pushed through her fear and shared pieces of her own story, the women were not judgmental, as she had long expected they would be. Feeling as though an initial balm had been applied to her heart, she found herself thanking God for Emily, and Harriet, and for this group. She knew she would keep coming.

———

"Hi Sadie, do you have a minute?" The meeting was over, and Sadie was making her way to the door when she heard Harriet behind her.

"Hi Harriet," she turned and smiled, "Thank you for tonight, it was really nice."

"Oh please, call me Hattie," she replied, touching her lightly on the arm then letting her hand fall. "I was really glad to see you here again tonight. When Emily called a few weeks ago to ask if she could register you, she mentioned that you might not be interested. I'm glad you were."

Sadie looked pensive and nodded, "She knew I needed this and I knew this was important to her." Sadie leaned in, "She also promised me ice cream after the first night to make sure I wouldn't bail."

Hattie chuckled, then asked, "It wasn't important for you too?"

"Uhh... not initially," Sadie wavered before continuing, "Like I said last week, it's been a few years for me now, and I was in a routine. Work, kids, hanging out with family, trying to make time for friends, but a piece of me was... is, missing. I think my plan was to try and just push through? I thought for a long time that this is just the new normal, but I know I'm not myself. Emily felt it too."

Hattie didn't rush to respond, and it made Sadie comfortable talking to her.

"I'm sorry to hear about your husband, I should have said so last week." Sadie said, quickly switching gears.

"Oh, thank you." She smiled, "He was just the best man. He had his quirks and there were times that he drove me batty, but I miss him every day." She waited a few seconds, looking like she was debating whether to continue. Then she did. "I know he's with Jesus now and on the really hard days that helps. Actually, it changes everything. I think he would be proud of me for pulling myself out of the slump I was in to move back home, and to be here for things like this. He was a model of patience, kindness, forgiveness... love. The Lord knows we wouldn't have made it all those years if he wasn't. He was the calm to my chaos."

"That's really nice..." Sadie smiled at her, but it didn't reach her eyes, her heart felt heavy. "I always wanted that kind of love. I thought that maybe I had it."

Hattie looked at Sadie with empathy. "Well, I'm glad you came back tonight. How did you find it? Any feedback for me?"

"It was lovely, really. You couldn't have done anything any better. Some of the stories that people shared were just heartbreaking. Mylanta. I mean, I knew I wasn't the only person to have ever gone through this, but it was more comforting than I thought it would be to actually see and hear that other people are feeling things that are similar to how I'm feeling. It's the guilt that I struggle with the most I think, and that's a hard thing to talk about. It pops up at the weirdest times, and just when you think that you're doing better, it comes around again."

"Yes, I can see how that would be."

"Last month was the first day of school for Tess and Jacob. They're 10 now and I had them all ready. It was their last first day of elementary school and leading up to the day I was feeling emotional myself, I just wanted to make sure they had a good day. I had their school supplies bought, new back-to-school outfits, new bookbags, new sneakers, home-made lunches- including star shaped cucumber slices. I even brought them to the beach the day before school started, to let them run and get all that extra energy out so that they would be tired enough at night that they would crash at home and get a good night's sleep. And they did! Came home and showered and then fell right into their beds. They woke up rested in the morning and were in great moods. I had everything ready by the door... so I'm feeling like 'yes, nailing this,' then we get to the school and I'm standing by my car in the drop off space watching them literally skip into the school together, and I look over and see other couples saying goodbye to their kids together and then this woman looked over at me with... so much judgement. It exuded from her. And this overwhelming feeling of sadness and guilt hit me. Logically I know that most kids take the bus to school, or only have one parent drop them off, but I spent the rest of the morning wondering if other kids at school were going to be talking about their dads. It ruined my morning."

Sadie stopped, realizing Hattie had only asked her how she felt the meeting had gone.

"I'm sorry Hattie. I guess I still get worked up sometimes. I feel like a mama bear who gets poked all the time. And I don't know when the poke is coming or who it's going to come from. I'm a bit on edge I guess."

"Oh Sadie, that's understandable. It does sound to me like the kids had a lovely back-to-school experience though." She was smiling, which wasn't the reaction Sadie had expected. "You know, I should tell you," Hattie continued, "you've just reminded me that once I had my boys, Albie used to call me 'Mamma' as a pet name all the time and it was simply one of my favorite names, it was short for Mamma Bear. He started using it when I would get defensive of one of the boys, and then it just stuck. I was always so protective of them, and heaven help the person who tried to talk to me about their antics." She leaned in whispering conspiratorially, "Those three little rascals could do no wrong in my eyes. I once told a neighbor that if she didn't stop getting after them for playing street hockey on THE STREET that I would be sending them all over to play in her driveway instead."

An unexpected laugh escaped from Sadie.

Hattie chuckled, shaking her head. "You know Sadie, if you didn't have something so precious to love, you wouldn't feel those pokes. To me, feeling the poke is a blessing."

Sadie thought about that for a second and knew that she would be thinking about it long after she left. Without thinking about it further, Sadie reached out and wrapped her arms around Hattie. "Thank you, Hattie."

"So about next week?" Hattie continued.

"I will come, and I will try to share more, but given that it's on creating future plans, I don't know how much I'll be able to contribute, I'm not sure I've figured that one out yet."

"And I think that's just the point my dear."

Chapter Twelve

Now

Fifteen minutes after the meeting ended Sadie was still talking with Hattie when she looked down at her watch and remembered that she had to leave to pick up Jacob at the rink. His U11 hockey team practice ended half an hour after her meeting at the church, which worked out perfectly.

The rain had stopped though there was still moisture in the air. Sadie pulled into the parking lot of the arena a few minutes early, and knowing Jacob would still be on the ice, she found a parking spot facing the front doors, turned off her car, and waited for his practice to end. After his first practice of the season a few weeks earlier, he asked her on the drive home if it would be ok with her if she stopped coming into the dressing room at the end of practice to help him take his skates off. He said he was old enough now to take them off on his own and could definitely change out of his gear by himself and pack it up on his own. She had watched him through the rearview mirror as she drove and could see the hope in his face as he asked. She had always loved seeing him right after practice- when his little cheeks were red and his hair was sweaty. She wanted to protest, but when he sensed her hesitation he quickly added that everyone on the team had decided that they could do it themselves this year and the coaches already offered to be there to help anyone who needed it. Given that, there wasn't much left to say. He said he'd still like her help tying his skates before practice which gave her a little reprieve from the fear that he was already getting too old for his mom.

Sadie was watching the doors of the arena open and close as parents, mostly dads, came out wheeling hockey bags or carrying their kid's gear over their shoulder, and she once again felt sad for Jacob who didn't have a dad around to carry his bag for him.

At her meeting tonight they talked about changing your self-talk and recommended looking for things to be thankful for when you weren't feeling that way. So tonight she decided to be purposefully thankful that her children were living in a town that was small but also offered enough amenities that they had things to do and activities to join when school was out. Jacob had been skating since he was a tot, and Tess was now in a ballet class, an activity she only began a couple of years ago, but very much enjoyed.

Sadie turned to look in the backseat double checking that her portfolio was still there. She reached for it and began flipping through the prints that she had pulled. The day before she had received a call from Levi Thompson, the Arena Manager, asking if she'd been willing to come by the arena at her convenience. He was looking to add some of her photographs to the lobby area as well as in the arena boardrooms. It was an opportunity that she was pretty excited about.

Sadie was the owner of Seaside Studios, a photography business that she had started while she was still in high school, which focused mainly on the East Coast culture and lifestyle. In the years since high school it had grown into a full blown studio and though you wouldn't hear her talk about it, her photographs were displayed in offices, lobbies and art galleries not just across the province, but across the country as well. Sadie had accomplishments that most would consider impressive, and it had all started off with a simple love of capturing images that others overlooked.

At 15, Sadie had developed the first set of pictures taken with her new camera. They were mostly of nature, taken on the path behind her home, and there had been a couple of Scarlett, when she had been focused on something other than Sadie's camera. The night she came down the stairs to show her parents her first set of pictures and ask them what they thought, Judy- Mason's mom, had been over visiting and she had taken a look as well.

"These are really good Sadie," she had said when she saw them "really, really good."

"You think?"

"Yes, sweetheart. I might get you to take some pictures of our family!"

What started off as a comment made in jest, turned into an hour the following week in the Gray's backyard, where Sadie took pictures of John, Judy, Mason, Jenny and Liam. While she took some traditional pictures of the five of them standing together in various poses, she also asked if she could take some pictures as they were just hanging around, before and after the shoot.

Later that week when she had them developed even she had been surprised at how good they were. When Judy and John looked through them the following night, Judy's eyes had welled up in tears at a picture Sadie had taken of her and John. Judy had been laughing at something he had just said to her, and in return he had pulled her into a hug. Sadie had taken the picture just as John had wrapped his arms around his wife to pull her in close. She was smiling up at him. When Sadie saw that picture for the first time, she had loved it too and had gone back to the photo lab to have it blown up larger and printed in black and white, their facial expressions had been so clear. Judy had immediately framed the photograph and she believed that it still hung in their family hallway to-day.

With the encouragement of her family, and Mason's, she spent much of her free time with a camera around her neck. At the beginning of the following lobster season, only a few months after Mason and Sadie had began dating, John asked her if she would be interested in coming with him to the wharf to take some pictures of Dumping Day. He was curious what would catch her eye and he was hopeful that she would take a picture that he could then hang in his office.

Darlings Lake sits on the peninsula of Southwest Nova Scotia and its local commercial lobster industry is the largest in Canada, the local fishing area one of the most productive in the world. Dumping Day is the first day of the lobster season, which in Darlings runs from late November to the end of May. While captains and crews make plans to dump their gear on the last Monday of November, they anxiously await the weather as a forecast of strong winds can delay the start of the season. The final call is made by the Department of Fisheries and Oceans and once the green light is given, nerves set in. Dumping Day is the most dangerous day of the lobster season. Captains have hundreds of traps on their vessel at one time, as well as all of their crew, and often a few extra men on board to support the work ahead. The weather in late November is cold and the mornings are dark, and despite having to be on the wharf before 5 AM to see your loved one off, it is a day that brings families and communities together like no other.

At each of the various harbours, friends, parents, siblings, spouses and children of all ages stand on wharves in hats, scarves and mittens calling 'I love you's', waving goodbye, and blowing kisses as the boats are untied and they begin their steam towards the work ahead. Families of one boat crew wish other captains and crews the best of luck, telling them to stay safe and also waving at them as well as they steam off. It's a strong community within a community, with everyone wanting the safety for all.

The first time Sadie experienced Dumping Day with John and Mason, it reminded her of the Who's in Whoville, families from all across the town waking up early to gather together to celebrate what was good, and in Nova Scotia, fishing was good. In Nova Scotia, the millionaires weren't in expensive restaurants and wearing suits and ties sitting behind nameplates on fancy desks. No in Nova Scotia, the millionaires sat next to you at the local pub, wearing rain boots and oil gear.

That first morning on the wharf, with only streetlamps and navigation lights from the fishing vessels to guide her, Sadie began taking pictures. She used her precision of skill to capture different elements of fishing that made it the successful industry that it was.

Away from view, she captured deckhands laughing and working together to ensure the boats had what they needed before taking off, wearing brightly colored oil gear that was wet and shiny. She zoomed in on colorful lobster traps piled high on the back of boats, or piled on land nearby, waiting to be picked up on the next load. She captured a grey-haired man, his back to her, wearing an old dirty beanie and picking up what looked to be his granddaughter as he wrapped her in a bear hug, her little hands tightened around his neck while her knitted mittens fell from her winter coat, hanging on only by strings. She came back the following week and took pictures of lobstermen being reunited with their families after long hauls offshore.

At her dad's encouragement, she submitted a couple of her pictures to the local newspaper and two of them were published the following day, including the one of the older fishermen with his granddaughter. John helped Sadie identify the man and when the season ended, Sadie returned with the photo framed as a gift. Unbeknownst to Sadie, he was a captain and he refused to take the gift without properly paying her. She had no idea what to charge him and after rifling through his wallet, he pulled out five hundred dollars and handed it to her. She was stunned and he said it was the least he could do. He told her his son and his granddaughter had been visiting that November from out west, and he knew he would cherish the picture forever. He was going to hang it in his wheelhouse.

The following year, in the weeks before Dumping Day, the newspaper editor sought Sadie out, asking her to take more pictures, and they were happy to pay her. She became a familiar face to the men and women who worked on the water and they shared a mutual admiration. Sadie of their work, and workers for capturing a unique glimpse into a life that few understood. Her dad insisted that she open a small business so that she could track her growth, take advantage of tax opportunities for young small business owners, and most importantly, to remind her that wherever she was, that she had so much to be proud of.

In Sadie's grade 12 year, she submitted a portfolio of both black and white and colored pictures depicting the intricacies of the lobster fishery of Southwest Nova Scotia, as well as pictures of people doing everyday tasks, to the University of Toronto as part of her application into their Visual Design program. It had earned her a phone call from a recruiter at the U of T, and after she hung up the phone and shared with her parents that the scholarship she had just been offered would cover all of her studies as well as most of her room and board for the full four-year program, they had both cried.

She remembered now as she flipped through her portfolio, that included a picture from that first Dumping Day, how she couldn't wait to run over and tell Mason about her scholarship. Mason Gray, the love of Sadie's life. She still couldn't believe that it hadn't worked out and she still couldn't understand why.

Just then the door to the arena flew open and the crack of the metal door against the building made Sadie lift her head. There was Jacob, running towards her car, red, sweaty and smiling. Sadie immediately started smiling, her son was a ball of energy, and she so enjoyed his company. He made her laugh all the time. She got out of the car and kneeled down to greet him with open arms. He flew into them, almost knocking her over as she laughed.

"Hey bud! How was practice?"

"It was awesome!" he responded, so excited to share with her. "I scored two goals and had one assist and Connor fell and hit his head and had to go sit on the bench. I don't know why he couldn't just keep playing, he had his helmet on. He still cries about everything, but that meant that *I* got to try to be goalie and coach said I did really good! And we have a new coach and he's so cool and..."

"Jacob, buddy, slow down." Sadie was laughing again. "Wait, where's your stuff?"

"Coach has it! He's bringing it out for me!"

Just then the door to the arena opened again and as Sadie looked up, she saw a tall, muscular man in track pants, a dark hoodie and a ball hat leave the arena. He was talking with Connor's dad and had Jacob's gear over his shoulder. She watched him nod bye to the man and then still to look around the parking lot. When he noticed Sadie and Jacob, he started the walk towards them.

She recognized that gait immediately and pairing it with his silhouette, felt the blood drain from her body. Her heart started racing, her knees went weak and her legs suddenly felt like jello. She had to put her hand on the ground to keep her balance.

"Hi, Sadie" said the familiar voice who had casually approached them.

She looked up and slowly stood, placing her hand on Jacob's shoulder for balance. "Mason."

He gave her a quick nod of the head, turning his attention briefly towards Jacob, "Here you go bud. Wanna go put these in the trunk?"

"Sure!" Jacob said, grabbing the handles of the oversized hockey bag from Mason, leaving Sadie to stand on her own volition.

"Jacob, wait in the car when you're done please." Sadie added.

"But why!?" Jacob pleaded, "I want to talk too!"

"No, I need to talk to your... coach... by myself."

Jacob sulked off and she could hear the trunk open behind her, but she couldn't take her eyes off of Mason.

"What's going on?" Sadie said, trying to keep her voice steady "Why... why are you here?"

He was watching her, concern etched on his face, "I'm coaching hockey."

She had forgotten what his voice sounded like, it was deeper than she remembered. She was having a hard time reconciling his voice and his face, which was covered in a light stubble. *Why did he still have to be so handsome?*

"I joined the team late." He continued, "I just moved back to the area and wanted to get involved."

"With *my* son's team?" She was incredulous.

"I didn't know he was going to be on the team Sade."

"Don't call me Sade!" Sadie snapped at him. "Don't do it."

"I'm sorry." He looked apologetic. "I can ask to help with another team, it's no problem."

She stared at him, her heart felt like it was slowly breaking all over again.

"Did you know he was going to be on the team when you signed up?'

"No, I didn't."

She believed him.

"I thought you were in Ontario." She responded. She knew she had to reconcile why he was here if she was ever going to sleep tonight.

"I was."

She was clearly waiting for more, so he took a deep breath and continued. "I got hurt last year on the ice, tore the ligaments in my knee and couldn't put on a pair of skates... for almost a year. I wasn't able to be the head coach I wanted to be and with more time than ever on the bench, it gave me a lot of time to think. I missed home more than I realized. Hockey wasn't working as a distraction anymore." He shrugged, "A couple of months ago when I called home, mom told me that dad had needed some help at work, said he was interviewing people to oversee his international operations and it didn't sit well with me, at all. I knew that I wanted that job, I wanted it to be me. I asked her to put dad on the phone and when I told him what I was thinking he stopped the whole process, hired me on the spot... It took me a little while to get everything sorted. I had to give notice to the team, all that stuff. But now it's done, and here I am. I'm living with mom and dad for now, while I figure out where in the area I want to buy."

She knew that Mason had started as an assistant coach with an American Hockey League team in Toronto when he was in his early twenties. She also knew that in recent years he'd been promoted to head coach. Scarlett had shared the news with her on facetime a couple of years ago. "Highest paid AHL coach in the country!" she had added enthusiastically.

"Seems like a big change."

"It is."

She didn't know what she was supposed to say to him now. 'See ya around' seemed insufficient.

"I was wondering," he started again, pulling his shoulders back. At just over 6 feet tall he stood much taller than her and when he looked down, his gaze was focused yet warm. "Would you like to get together some night? Or in the day, if that's easier."

Her heartbeat that had slowed, started to pick up again. "Mason."

He waited and watched her, not in a rush to fill in the silence. He was only a couple of feet away from her, if she wanted to reach out and touch him she could.

"I don't know if that's a good idea." She finally responded.

He waited, mulling that over.

"I miss you Sadie." He said finally, never one to mince words, "And I'd like to hear about how you and the kids have been doing since Nick left."

Chapter Thirteen

Then

The night of Sadie's 15th birthday, just after 11PM, Caroline Campbell watched her oldest daughter walk with Mason up the hill from the campfire towards her car. She had told Judy she would drive both kids home, saving her friend the drive. Sadie looked beautiful, her mother thought watching her climb the hill, certainly much more confident and surer of herself than Caroline had been at that age .

In the last few months, she had watched Sadie really begin to come into her own and she couldn't have been more proud of her. She was a good daughter- she had really given her and Stephen no problems at all. She was also a strong student- more organized than what was reasonable for a teenager, a good friend to those she loved, and much to Caroline's delight, she loved Jesus. This new love that Sadie had for photography exuded from her. She couldn't wait to see what she would do with that passion, to watch it develop. She was kind to Scarlett, most of the time, and yet still had a youthfulness to her that Caroline appreciated and knew she would miss as Sadie got older.

In summers prior, Sadie and Scarlett had always attended two weeks of camp and whenever possible, Caroline had always signed them up to go the same week, not only was she comforted knowing they had each other should one of them start to feel homesick, but it also allowed her and Stephen to have the house to themselves, a rare opportunity that they- especially Stephen, had always looked forward to.

But Sadie was signed up for seven weeks this summer, which was pretty much her full break from school, and Caroline was having a hard time with it. Knowing that the work experience and opportunities to spend the summer with her friends was a positive thing, it didn't cancel out the fact that Caroline had loved spending summer days with her girls, and this year would be different. And even though she knew Sadie would be home on weekends, she also knew how tiring being a camp counsellor was and she expected Sadie to want to relax or sleep most of the time she was home.

Caroline had tried being a counsellor herself once, the summer she was 17, and hadn't made it through the summer. Camp was too much sun and not enough sleep, too much energy exerted and not enough food or breaks to make up for it, too many loud kids hyped up on sugar and not enough quiet time to do other things she had enjoyed in the summer- going to the beach, reading in her hammock, and hanging out driving around with her friends. She had called it after her first week and picked up a day job babysitting instead.

She knew from the get-go that Sadie was different and would be able to handle it. She had always loved camp and attended a camp leadership training session for a weekend last summer, just so she would qualify to work there this summer. After camp confirmed that she was hired, she had spent hours in her room memorizing a 10-minute melody of songs that the Director had given her in the Spring. It was going to kick-off the daily sing-a-long time with the campers, and staff were expected to know it so that they could work together to come up with actions during the first week of staff training. All of it was time and preparation that she doubted parents of the campers realized teenagers put in so that their kids would have a great week at camp. And don't even get her started on the pay. They worked for pennies, and though it was meant to be a ministry, these kids were passing up other better paying jobs to be there. Caroline had already planned to make sure that when Sadie arrived home each weekend this summer her room would be clean and her favorite foods would be waiting for her in the fridge.

The night before Sadie left for her first week of camp training, Caroline had knocked on her bedroom door, wanting to spend some time with her oldest daughter before she left for most of the summer. Sadie had been listening to music which had blocked out the sound of Caroline's knock. Caroline had slowly opened the door, hoping not to startle her, she caught her eye and smiled as Sadie quickly pulled down her headphones and clicked the stop on her Walkman, removing the headphones from around her neck.

Sadie welcomed her into her room but didn't seem at all aware that Caroline was missing her so much already. She was talking a mile-a-minute about how excited she was to be gone for the summer and how much fun she planned to have. The feeling of missing Sadie intensified when Sadie called a few weeks later asking if she could spend the evening of her 15th birthday at camp. Caroline had been heartbroken. Unbeknownst to Sadie, when Caroline had realized her birthday fell on a Friday she had gone ahead and made plans at the local spa for them that evening. Hearing the combination of excitement and trepidation in Sadie's voice when she had called to ask her about staying, she knew the spa date could easily be postponed to another time. It was a blessing, Caroline knew, to have her daughter so happy where she was and Stephen was the one she would share her sadness with, not Sadie.

Caroline had asked her that night as they chatted and packed, whether or not there were any boys at camp that she was interested in and she had immediately responded that no, definitely not, but Caroline hadn't really had to ask. Without realizing it, for the past few weeks Sadie had been casually mentioning Mason's name around the house, at times that he normally wouldn't have come up. When she had asked to go to Mason's house after she opened up her new camera, Caroline heard the back door slam and had said to her husband then, 'Mark my words Stephen, those two might begin dating very soon.' He had brushed it off and told her that she had read one too many romance novels and was getting ahead of herself, but Caroline had a mothers' instinct that her husband did not.

She had mentioned her suspicions to Judy just last week when she had stopped into her house for coffee and to commiserate about missing her girl, when Judy had enthusiastically agreed, confiding that she had been noticing the same thing with Mason as well. The women had promised each other that they wouldn't get their hopes up, but they both knew they were empty words said in vain. The hopes were already up. Heavens, they had each been to visit the other in the hospital when the babies were born- the Gray's a second family to the Campbell's, and vice versa. The women had talked about this when they were young, overtired moms- about how fun it would be if someday they actually ended up as family, but at that time it was just a fantasy between friends.

Now though, as Caroline watched how Mason was looking at Sadie as they approached her car, there was really no question how much he adored her daughter. Caroline loved Mason, and Jenny and Liam too, as if they were her own. She knew Mason had a strong faith in God and trusted that should they actually begin dating, that he would treat her respectfully. The only concern that had really surfaced when she had thought about it for any amount of time, was what would happen to their families' friendship if for some reason they began dating and then things went south, but in that case Stephen was right, she was getting ahead of herself.

Caroline was bewildered when instead of getting in the front seat, Sadie moved to get into the back seat with Mason for the drive home. She had always sat in the front with Caroline and without anyone having to say anything, Caroline knew something had changed. She put on a smile and turned to wish Sadie a Happy Birthday, told her she couldn't believe her girl was 15.

While she didn't want to verbalize her observation that Sadie was sitting in the back seat, which she knew would make the situation more awkward for them- she had a thousand and a half questions that she was dying to ask. At the risk of embarrassing anyone, she opted not to say anything about it at all, and to help prevent her from blurting out her magnitude of questions, quick thinking resulted in her reaching forward and turning up the car radio instead. She was thankful that Tubthumping by Chumbawama had just started playing. Because Scarlett and Stephen had been playing it around the house, and though the song drove her nutty (she found it very inappropriate), she now knew most of the words.

Her shock of seeing Sadie get in the backseat resulted in an unexpected combination of events. Caroline, who was wearing matching pajamas and sitting in the front seat alone, found herself driving in the dark and chanting quite loudly about how she got knocked down, and up again, how you're never gonna keep her down. Panicked at how the drive was unfolding yet unable to stop singing, her yelling suddenly turned into an operatic melody about how she was pissing the night away. She couldn't even stop herself. Luckily the song only lasted three and a half minutes and when it was over she dared glance in the review mirror to find Sadie looking at Mason, in horror. Caroline was relieved to see that he was grinning back. Unfortunately for Sadie, music was a great distraction to Caroline's thoughts, so she continued to keep the music turned up until they pulled into Mason's driveway.

"Goodnight Mason." Caroline finally found her speaking voice.

"Goodnight Caroline," Mason smiled at her, "Thank you very much for the drive."

Mason reached for the back door handle, as did Sadie on her side, both leaving the inside of the car to walk towards the back of it. Caroline popped the trunk so Mason could grab his suitcase and waited anxiously in the front seat for Sadie to get back in. A minute after hearing the trunk close,

Caroline was still sitting alone in the car. The kids had moved and she could see them now through her side rearview mirror and she watched as Mason wrapped his arms around Sadie, bringing her into a tight hug. They talked only for a few more seconds before Sadie turned and started towards the opposite side of the car, opening the front door and looking at her mom for the first time since she'd been picked up.

"Good birthday?" Caroline asked, glancing at Sadie, one hand on the wheel and the other on the back of Sadie's headrest as she began to back down the driveway.

"It really was." Sadie looked flushed, "Most of it anyway."

"Oh yeah, do you wanna talk about it?" Caroline wondered if maybe she had misread the situation.

"Do *you* wanna talk about it?" Sadie asked her mom.

"What do you mean, why wouldn't I?"

"Pissing the night away! Really Mom!? At full blast!?"

Caroline shook her head, her eyebrows furrowed. "Come on now Sadie. It sounds like you need.." then switching to a sing-song voice in her best English accent, "a song that reminds you of the good times. A song that reminds you of the better times!"

Sadie turned to her mom and after a couple of seconds, bent over at the waist and started giggling. It reminded Caroline of when Sadie was just a little girl, she had always bent over when she laughed.

"Mom! I can't believe you. How do you even know that song?!"

"I know. I panicked. I'm so sorry." They were both laughing now. "Wait until dad hears."

Sadie was still smiling, now looking out of her window and up at the stars.

"But really, do you want to talk about... everything?" Caroline asked a few moments later as she pulled into their driveway.

"Yeah, but not until tomorrow if that's ok?"

"Sure thing kiddo," she said. "I can't wait."

"Me too."

Sadie grabbed her bag from the trunk and once in the house, started straight for her room. Caroline said goodnight as Sadie walked down the hall, letting her know that they would do cake and gifts tomorrow as a family when everyone was home. Sadie said that sounded great and that she was so sorry but that she was wiped and wanted to go to bed.

Caroline replied 'of course' and hid her disappointment as she watched the back of her daughter's curled hair as Sadie opened her bedroom door and slipped into her room. She had looked so lovely tonight, Caroline thought again as she heard the door to her daughter's room click as it closed.

This was going to be a new season for all of them and Caroline for one, couldn't wait for the next day to hear directly from Sadie all about her week, and about the boy-next-door who had captured her heart.

Chapter Fourteen

Then

Hearing the news that summer that Sadie and Mason had begun dating had been a shock only to Sadie's dad Stephen. Everyone else in their families had seen it coming, and when the kids began to share the news within their circle of friends, their friends had been excited for them, adding a lot of 'Well it's about time!'s and other variations of 'Shocker!'. Emily, Scarlett and Rachel had been the happiest for Sadie, which made sense, given they were her closest friends.

The morning after Sadie's 15th birthday and her first kiss, Sadie asked her parents if they had some time to talk, which they both did. She sat down with them in their living room and very nervously asked them what they would think if she and Mason began... dating.

"You've got to be kidding me." Stephen had responded, while Caroline turned and gave him a sympathetic look. She placed her hand on his leg and didn't have to say anything else. He later conceded that yes, she had been right.

Caroline had responded to Sadie that yes of course, that would be fine- they loved Mason and that they were very happy for her. Caroline didn't last a minute on the couch where she had been sitting next to Stephen, before she got up and moved to sit next to Sadie, grabbing her daughter's hands in her own. Stephen watched, quietly observing two of the women he loved the most in the world, thankful that Caroline seemed to know how to handle these situations.

"You can't be alone with him." It was the first phrase he managed to fit in a few minutes later, with the girls rattling on as they were. Caroline paused and looked at him, confused, and then her heart swelled. Of course he was nervous. She knew he had a fierce love for his daughters and only wanted to keep them safe, years as an RCMP officer had opened his eyes to dangers within the world and he had always erred on the side of overprotection.

"What he means," Caroline continued, "is that there will have to be some new rules now, now that you're dating."

"Nope, not really what I meant at all," Stephen huffed.

She smiled at him and turned back to Sadie. "I will talk to Judy and we will just all have to be on the same page in terms of ground rules... Like, no being alone together in your room, or his."

Stephen made a sudden coughing sound and Caroline continued, ignoring him. "There's really no need to be in each other's bedrooms anyway -if you want to hang out alone or watch a movie you can do it in our family rooms. You'll need a curfew for when you go out, and, well Sade, we just... we just," her throat felt like it was closing as tears sprang to her eyes, "I can't believe you have a boyfriend. My baby." She leaned in and hugged her daughter, holding her close.

Judy and John had been on the same page as Caroline and Stephen in terms of creating boundaries and expectations for their children and really, very little changed in the years following the initial announcement, aside from how much the two hung out together. They had stayed working at camp Hope for the remainder of that first summer, which had been fun, but also something Sadie found hard. She had just wanted to spend all of her free time with Mason but there were strict rules at camp that didn't allow them to hang around together alone at all, so while they snuck out of their cabins a few times after lights-out to steal a kiss or tell each other a story, there was very little time for them to have any long conversation unless someone else was around. They would often manage to brush hands when they walked by each other, but it was early into their relationship when Sadie was already wondering if this is how it was going to be, if camp was going to be on the table the following summer.

They had loved the week in between camp ending and school starting, when they got to just be together and hold hands and talk. They walked the beach and talked about what they thought Darlings High would be like, excited to be starting grade 10 together as a couple.

Once school started, they continued to have meals at each other's houses, only this time, without both full families there. Through the school year they spent a lot of time together watching movies, doing homework and hanging around with their siblings, and they both loved attending church and Youth Group together. They each also had friends and interests of their own, which their parents thought they had done a good job of balancing.

Mason continued to play competitive hockey and made the Junior A hockey team the first year he was eligible to try out. He practiced a few nights a week, one morning a week, and played most weekends from September to March, travelling across the province and even into nearby provinces for away games. Sadie rarely missed a home game and while he often travelled with the team that first year he played, when she could, Sadie would join his parents for the away games. She loved cheering him on and while some of the guys on the team gave him a hard time about it, he loved looking up from the ice and seeing her in the stands. When the season ended, to earn spending money he helped his dad out at his work whenever he could, his dad always having something for him to do.

Sadie continued to take pictures, and began receiving calls, first from people in her community, and then from people outside of it, asking if she'd be willing to take someone's family pictures, or pictures of their newborn baby. She always said yes. After her dad helped her open her business, she worked with a lady from church who had volunteered to help her keep her books, and she had explained to Sadie the process to follow when she wanted to make new purchases for the business, or take out spending money of her own.

———

In the Spring of their grade 10 year, Sadie and Mason and 12 other kids from their youth group had been on their way home from a trip to Cape Breton when Mason received a message that nothing was wrong, but that he'd needed to call his dad as soon as he could. They had been stopped at a McDonald's for supper and Mason had been leaving the restaurant with his friend Jake when the youth leader called him over, handed him his Motorola cell phone, and relayed the message. Mason took the call by himself leaning behind the brick building where no one could see him, his left foot pressed on the wall behind him. If nothing was wrong, he couldn't imagine what couldn't wait until tonight at midnight when the vans were due to arrive home.

After a couple of rings, his dad picked up. "Hello?"

"Hey dad, what's up?"

"Hey Mase. Where are you?"

"At a McDonalds in Sydney, everyone's just finishing up and Jake and I got done early. What a great trip, wait till I tell you about..."

His dad uncharacteristically interrupted him, "Mase, I need to tell you something."

"Sure," Knowing nothing was wrong, he didn't know what could possibly be so urgent, "What's up?"

His dad took a deep breath. "Your mother and I received a phone call today... from the London Knights."

Mason thought he felt his heart skip a beat and he pulled away from the building, beginning to pace on the spot.

"I'm sorry... what?"

"The head coach from the Knights called Mason. They want you to play for them next year."

"That's impossible."

"It's not son. They've seen your stats from the season, footage of you playing, they want you to play for them. They want to choose you as their first draft pick."

"I'm not even eligible for the draft!" Mason was starting to panic. He knew that looking at numbers alone, that even though he was one of the youngest players, he was the best forward on his team, but he had never compared his stats to players on other teams. Who really cared about that? He played hockey for fun. He truly loved it. But he also loved living in Darlings. He loved Sadie.

"You are eligible Mason. We just didn't talk about it as it seemed so unlikely." His dad could sense Mason's panic and remained calm.

"I can't though Dad, I'm still in school."

"Well, that's what we have to talk about. They've said that you can do your grade eleven year there, in Ontario. They've said they will arrange a family for you to stay with, but your Aunt Linny and Uncle Jack are nearby too, I'm sure if you wanted to, you could stay with them. They'd love that."

"Do you want me to go?" Mason was so confused. This had never even been a light conversation over dinner. But... the OHL? Playing in the Ontario Hockey League was a HUGE deal. One other kid from Darlings was drafted to the OHL about 10 years prior and he was now playing in the NHL, it was something Mason had never even dared hoped for.

"I want you to go if you want to go, yes, absolutely."

"But Sadie Dad, what about Sadie?"

There was a long pause on the other end of the line.

"Dad?"

"God knows the plans he has for you Mason. Remember Jeremiah 29. Now, whether it includes the OHL, or whether it is staying home, that I don't know. You'll need to pray about it and this is why I'm calling you now. They've asked that you give them a call on Tuesday to let them know your decision.

If you decline, they will give the spot to someone else. It's already Sunday. The draft is going to be announced publicly on Friday. I wanted to give you as much time as you can to think about it and pray about it."

"What would you do?" His voice broke and he could feel his heart racing. He knew even as he was asking his dad that it was unfair. Neither John nor Judy had ever pressured Mason when it came to hockey. He knew his dad loved watching him play, but playing better, playing harder, perfecting his skills- none of it had ever become all-consuming for their family like he knew it had for parents of other players on his team.

"I don't know. If you want to play hockey at a higher-level son, this is the best opportunity, and it might not come around again. If you have no interest in that, then you just need to be comfortable saying no. But I can't tell you what to do. I won't. But you need to know Mason, I love you so much. So does your Mother. We'll support you however we can."

"Can I talk to mom?"

"She's gone out right now. She'll be sad she missed your call. She only cried for an hour after the coach called." He chuckled, "she misses you already. She thinks you'll want to go, but we trust in the Lord and know he has plans for you buddy- whatever they may be."

"Can I tell Sadie? And Jake?"

"You can tell anyone you want, it's not a secret, but if I could offer some advice," He paused, choosing his words carefully, "I think you need to keep it to yourself, for today anyway. I want you to think about what *you* really want, not what someone else wants for you, whatever that may be. It's your life- your school year, your living arrangements, your future. I don't want to see you swayed by someone else's opinions of what decision you should make, even Sadie. You are not married Mason, as a reminder, you can make this decision all on your own. Now tomorrow, tomorrow I would talk to her. You can weigh what she says against how you're leaning."

"Ok, thanks Dad. That makes sense... I can't, I can't believe it."

"I know," John was smiling though Mason couldn't see it, "I'm so proud of you. So so proud."

"Thanks Dad. I'll see you when I get home? Who's picking us up?"

"I am tonight, I'll see you around midnight. I love you bud."

"I love you too dad. Thanks for calling."

"Of course. We'll chat later."

And with that, Mason hung up just as Sadie and Emily were rounding the corner.

Sadie looped her arms around Mason and looked up at him smiling. "Found you! Jake said your dad called. Is everything ok?"

"Yeah, yeah, everything's fine. We just confirmed the pickup time for tonight."

Mason felt her give him another quick squeeze before she let go. He loved this girl so much. There was nothing he wouldn't do for her. She wasn't just his girlfriend, she was his best friend. She made him laugh all the time and when he watched her talking to anyone else, he was so proud that he was the one that got to date her. He couldn't wait to marry her someday. He had never mentioned it to her, that would really freak her out, but he knew without a doubt that one day she would really be his.

Mason took his dad's advice and didn't mention the details of the call he'd just received to anyone else. It was starting to get dark out and as he climbed in the backseat of the van, he grabbed his Walkman and a spot next to the window, lifting his arm so Sadie could snuggle in next to him. It was easy to pretend to be tired- it had been a long day, so that's what he did. He gave his girlfriend a kiss on the forehead and as she put her own Walkman on and closed her eyes, he stared out of the window, smiling to himself. Because as much conviction as he felt in how much he loved Sadie, he also had the same conviction that by this time next year, he will have completed his first season in the OHL.

Chapter Fifteen

Now

Sadie had been in a trance for the entirety of the drive home and didn't hear much of what Jacob had been saying as he talked a mile-a-minute from the backseat about the ins and outs of his practice, every observation he had made on the ice. She was thankful his energy and stories were keeping him too distracted to notice that she hadn't been engaging.

How long had Mason been home for? Why hadn't she seen him? And more importantly, why hadn't anyone told her he was home!? Her parents must have known. Surely Emily had heard. No one had thought to even text her? And was she just supposed to what, go out to dinner with him? Really!? A decade after they broke up?

Sadie pulled into her driveway, took Jacob's gear out of the trunk and set it inside her garage. He grabbed his sticks and ran inside, swinging the front door wide open and yelling for his Grammy and Grampy who were inside waiting for them. Her parents had agreed to watch Tess this evening while her and Jacob were out, and even though her head was spinning, she was happy they were there. Even though they lived only a 20-minute drive away, her business and kids kept her busy and she didn't see them as much as she wanted to.

The smell of freshly baked cookies hit her as soon as she walked through the door and a feeling of nostalgia washed over her. Her mom had been a stay-at-home mother for the entirety of her childhood and her skills in the kitchen were, in Sadie's opinion, unmatched. Caroline had taken great joy in baking for her family and Sadie and Scarlett had known that they could count on homemade bread, cookies or muffins each day after school. She could hear that Jacob had already made his way to the kitchen to find his grandmother.

Nick had left just over 5 years ago now, walking away from any interest he had in the house they had bought together shortly before they had been married. Back then Nick hadn't been making much money and Sadie had always leaned conservative in her spending, so the house was modest given what she could afford now, but it suited the three of them perfectly. A small three-bedroom cottage tucked off the road had been what she was looking for. And while it wasn't on the water, it was on a small, manicured lot surrounded by trees which had helped sell Sadie on the location. She loved being in nature and knew her favorite place would be sitting out on the back deck, which it had been.

Sadie made her way into the kitchen and towards her mom who was doing a better job of listening to Jacob than she had done. Her mom gave her a wide-eyed look over Jacob's head and Sadie chuckled, grabbed a warm cookie off the cookie sheet and leaned in to give her mom a kiss on the side of the head. Then, she went looking for her dad.

She found him at the edge of his seat watching the Blue Jays game. Growing up, she couldn't count the number of baseball games she'd seen her parents watch together and as Sadie got older, the team had slowly etched its place on her life as well. The team's schedule was printed and hung on her fridge, she knew the personalities of the players and most of their background stories. From April to September other tv shows lost their appeal and regularly scheduled programming took a backseat. It was the end of September now though, and the Blue Jays were still in it, sitting at the top of their division with only a week to go, and looked to be making a real run at a playoff spot. It had been years since that had happened and no one in Canada was more excited than her dad. He loved the team with a passion that Sadie thought might actually be driving him crazy. He wasn't much of a communicator, preferring decompressing over talking, yet she always knew how the team was doing by how he was sitting- either at the edge of his seat or laid back and cursing under his breath.

She took the seat across from him. The room was cozy. Her mother had dimmed the living room lights and had a candle going on a side table. She noticed her laundry had been taken off the line and folded, it was sitting in a clothing basket at the end of her couch. It was hard to ever be upset with them when she knew how much they loved her and wanted to take care of her.

"8-5 in the ninth! Nice." Sadie observed, "They'll take this one."

"They will. This is the year Sadie. I can feel it in my bones." Her dad hadn't looked in her direction, but no offense was taken.

"You've been saying that my whole life Dad." Sadie laughed, pulling her knees up and tucking her feet under her, wrapping her arms around her legs, like she used to sit when she was younger.

"But I mean it this time. This is the team that can do it."

"I just don't want to get my hopes up." Sadie replied.

Her father scoffed at her and then suddenly clapped his hands loudly. Two outs, bottom of in the ninth and the batter from the other team swung and missed on a full count. Game over.

"Ah ha!" He exclaimed and finally looked at her, beaming. He muted the TV as the team celebrated. She smiled at her dad, his dark hair had turned mostly grey in the last few years, the wear and tear from his job starting to show. He was looking older lately, more tired. She made another mental note to make sure to spend more time with her parents.

"So..." Sadie said, tilting her head and looking at her dad.

"So... what?" He looked back at her.

"Mason's home?"

"Ah, yes. I heard that." Her father set down the remote.

"Dad. He pretty much lives next door to you. Judy and John didn't tell you?"

"No, they did."

"And you didn't think to tell me?" She asked, unconvinced.

"Why would I tell you?"

"What do you mean?"

"What do you mean, what do I mean?" Now Stephen was confused.

"Dad!"

"What!?"

"Nobody told me."

"I don't understand Sadie. Why would we tell you?"

She stared at him and was suddenly embarrassed. She realized that he was right. Why would he tell her? This is someone she dated for a few years in high school and she hadn't brought him up since that time, not to her parents anyway. Her father couldn't possibly know how much she had loved him or the extent of the pain she felt when they had broken up.

"Ok, never mind." Sadie conceded. "I just saw him tonight and it took me by surprise, that's all. It had been a long time."

Her dad nodded, but didn't say anything else. A man of few words. She loved it most of the time and other times it drove her batty.

She noticed her mom then, standing in the doorway looking contrite. Her mom had overheard the conversation and couldn't play coy on this one, Sadie knew that her mom could've easily guessed how Sadie would feel knowing Mason Gray was back in town. She looked over at her mom but didn't say anything, her eyes suddenly welling with unshed tears.

"I'm sorry Sadie. I'm really sorry, I should have said something."

Stephen looked between his wife and his daughter, "What in the world?" He shook his head and stood, leaving to find his grandson, someone he understood.

"Why didn't you say something?" Sadie asked. She wasn't mad anymore, just curious, a bit sad. Her mom came and took the seat where her father had been sitting.

"I only found out last week. Judy came over for a visit and she wanted me to know, she was actually wondering if she should text you to let you know. I told her that that was really nice, but no, I would tell you, and then I could never find the right time. I didn't know what to say, 'Hi honey, just wanted you to know that the boy that you loved for years, that one who broke your heart is living right back with his parents next door. He's single and strong and looks like a tall glass of water on a hot day. Hope all is well!'"

"Mom." Sadie grinned.

"Well, really. I didn't know what to say. Or how you would react."

"I don't know how I'm reacting. He did look good. He's Jacob's hockey coach now."

"Oh really?" Her mom raised her eyebrows.

"Yeah. We only talked for a minute, and then when I was leaving he asked if he could take me out."

"Really." Her mom didn't look at all surprised by this.

"Yeah."

"And what did you say?"

"I said absolutely not! I can't go out with Mason again!"

"Oh, ok."

"What?"

"Nothing."

"Mom! What?" Sometimes when she talked to her parents she unintentionally reverted to her teenage mannerisms, she knew she had to work on that too.

"I just... well... I guess I just don't see what the harm would be. I'm sure he just wants to talk. Maybe it will help heal something in you."

"A breakup from forever ago is not something I want to rehash."

"No, but what you want to do, and what you should do for yourself, may be two different things."

Sadie thought about that for a second, her heart rate picking up speed- in a race, trying to catch up to her brain.

"You don't think that would be weird?"

"What? No. You're both adults."

"But I'm a divorced adult."

"Yes, dear. I know. And despite what you might think, you still have the right to eat dinner with another man, or have coffee, or go do whatever it is he wants to do." She looked at her daughter again, this time with a little mischief in her eyes.

Sadie's eyes widened as she caught the innuendo.

"You're unbelievable." And then, her brain catching up, "how do you know he's single?"

"Judy may have mentioned it when she was over."

Sadie quietly sat on that as her mom stood, coming over and placing her hand on Sadie's shoulder. She looked down at her daughter. "I love you very much. I want to see you happy. You've been alone for many years now and if you want to have coffee with Mason, you should. If you don't honey- then don't. You have so much good in your life, but... I know my girl. And I know that something has a hold of you."

She leaned down and kissed the top of Sadie's head. "Tess helped me with the cookies and we had a great night. She's excited about her dance recital coming up. She told me she got the part of a mouse in the Nutcracker? She's very excited about it. She's in her room watching YouTube videos of the dances." Then added conspiratorially, "Do I have to go?"

Sadie laughed. "Yeah, I think we all do."

Her mother gave her a look of panic then quickly added, "anything for my girl... my girls."

A few minutes later after tight hugs all around, her parents were headed to their car. Jacob and Tess changed into their pajamas and after brushing their teeth, Sadie went in and kissed them each goodnight, letting them know they could read for the next half hour and then lights out.

Once again thankful for her mother tidying up, Sadie changed into her own pajamas and made her way to the kitchen to take up her mother's departing suggestion of a warm cookie with a glass of milk before bed.

She grabbed her favourite fall mug and poured her milk into it, placing it in the microwave. As she stood there, hearing the low hum kick in as it slowly spun her cup, she watched the glass plate rotate, contemplating in her quiet kitchen how one action can cause something to change the nucleus of what it was meant to be. One conversation and a three-year relationship is over. One night with a man and a new life is formed, one meaningful statement from your mom and the penitence you've wrapped around yourself like a tight blanket begins to loosen, one press of a button and your milk goes from cold to... warm. The beeping of the microwave pulled Sadie from her thoughts.

She hadn't truly considered saying yes to Mason, but now that she's talked to her mom, maybe her mom was right. Maybe it would be good for her, important even, to talk with Mason. She was pretty sure it couldn't make anything worse. Deep down she knew she wouldn't be able to fool herself for long. She had never wanted to be apart from him. To talk to him now, to hear his laugh... she shook her head. They didn't even know each other anymore. She worried there was too much history between them now. She worried about what he would think of her, she worried about what other people would think, she worried about what her kids would think. She worried about a lot of things, she thought, sighing. But her mom had always seemed to know what Sadie needed, even when she couldn't see it for herself. She had 32 years of examples of that. *What if she is right about this too?*

Chapter Sixteen

Then

Mason was lying on his bed, staring at the ceiling. Glancing at his clock for the 25th time in five minutes, he knew that Sadie would be bouncing through the door any minute, excited to see him, thinking that they were going to be finalizing plans for their move to Ontario in two weeks' time. His heart was racing and he didn't feel good. He rolled over to his side and thought he might actually be sick. He felt dizzy and lightheaded and was dreading the conversation that he was about to have with her. He was going to end things with Sadie Campbell, the girl he had been in a relationship with for the past three years and had probably always loved.

Looking around his room he saw mementos of her everywhere. To the right of his bedroom doorway next to his hockey sticks were three large glass-framed collages hanging vertically in white wooden frames. Each year on their dating anniversary Sadie had given him pictures from their year together. It was his favorite gift to open each year, she always managed to choose the photos that brought him the most joy- significant events in each of their individual lives, photos of them together and photos they had taken of each other without the other knowing, usually mid-laugh or doing something silly. The middle collage was of their second year together and she had included in it a picture of him signing his OHL contract. It's funny how one picture can bring such joy and also such apprehension.

He had been so nervous that Spring back in grade 10, to tell her about his opportunity to go to Ontario for his grade 11 year, to play in the OHL. She had reacted pretty much like how he had expected her to. She loved him and so of course was happy for him, but they had also spent a lot of time talking about how scared she was about how little time they'd get to spend together, logistics on how'd they stay in touch, her fear of him meeting and falling in love with someone else. He thought that last part was ridiculous. He had spent the next few months patient with her, reassuring her, and he remembered now telling her that the only way he could prove to her that everything was going to be ok, was for him to actually go so that he could call her, or write to her, and show her how excited he would be to see her on his trips home. She had wanted to trust him at face value, but he knew she had struggled in convincing her heart.

Not long after he and Sadie had started dating, he decided that he wasn't going to go back and work at Camp Hope the following summer. As much as he loved it, he had become really interested in his grade 10 business classes and had been doing really well in them, he could relate everything that he was learning to his dad's business, and he wanted to spend the summer working with his dad, learning even more. He had expected Sadie would go back to camp, but as a result of him deciding to play in the OHL, she gave up her summer position at Camp Hope so that she could spend more time with him, even if just in the evenings. She had mentioned Rachel and camp to him so much that summer that it had ended up becoming a tension point between them. He hadn't asked her not to go back to camp, and didn't like feeling guilty that she was missing out on something that she loved. She had just wanted him to acknowledge that she chose him over camp.

Though the tension was like a flood tide that summer, building slowly and surely, it had released quickly, an ebb of emotion washed away when they finally sat down on his parents porch swing late one August evening to talk about how they had each been feeling. When they shared their feelings, they were relieved to realize it had all been rooted in the fact that they cared about each other so much. He wanted her to be happy, she was willing to sacrifice what she loved to be with him. They had made a commitment that first year to always be honest with each other and to make a date on the porch swing if something was starting to bother them. Many discussions had been had over the past three years on that swing. It looked out over the lake that both of their families had homes on. Only a small number of their discussions on the swing were related to issues they had to work through, most nights were spent recapping their days- how school was going and her of her photography clients and upcoming projects, him of how hockey was going and what it was like being away. They shared funny stories, planned for their future, shared their dreams.

This year Mason had been home visiting when the first snow fell, and they had met on the swing to watch it together, they spent the evening holding hands under a blanket, slowly rocking back and forth, wearing touques and talking about getting through the rest of the school year when they would both finally be graduated from High School and Sadie could join him in Ontario. As the porch lights came on and darkness fell, Sadie had fallen asleep on his shoulder and he couldn't remember being happier.

That was only a few months ago. Now, as Mason's eyes moved from the collages, they landed on the first gift she had ever bought him, a sweater to replace the first one she had borrowed, the one she was wearing when they had their first kiss. She had kept it and through a light-hearted apology told him he wasn't ever getting it back, it was hers now. But every now and then she had asked him to wear it for at least a day so that it would continue to smell like him. 'My favorite smell' she had said once, making him blush, but he felt the same about her.

He pressed the palms of his hands over his eyes and tried to take deep breaths, he didn't want to cry. He was going to be leaving Nova Scotia in two weeks, but he wasn't going to Ontario anymore, not like Sadie thought he was. Mason had received another life-changing call last week, this time with an offer to sign him to a One-Way AHL contract. He would be playing full time for a team in British Columbia, and if he performed like he hoped he would, he could be called up to the NHL. British Columbia was over a forty-hour drive, or a five-hour flight from Ontario and Mason could not, would not, put Sadie through another four years of a long distance relationship. She struggled with long distance. He did too, but while he had hockey and training and games to keep him busy, Sadie didn't. She spent a lot of time missing him and calling him and all he had heard all summer was how excited she was to finally be in the same province, the same school as him. And there was simply no way that Mason could ask her to come to BC with him, to give up a full scholarship at the University of Toronto, in a program that she loved. That would be so selfish. He knew how much she needed that scholarship, how much it had meant to her family. No, Mason knew he had to put Sadie first, even if she didn't understand it yet, even if it might actually kill him.

Mason had thought it all through. He had prayed about it, and even though he hadn't received the clear direction he had hoped he would, no other option made more sense to him. He hadn't talked to his parents about his decision. He didn't want them to try and sway him. No, he was no longer a kid, he needed to step up and make the best decision for him and for Sadie. In his mind, he was releasing Sadie from another long-distance relationship. She could go to the U of T and focus fully on school. She wouldn't be spending her free time writing to him, or calling him, or driving to him, or sitting on flights. She could focus on photography, the thing that she loved and was so amazingly talented at. That was the thing that mattered, and if, at the end of university, she still wanted to be with him, then they would absolutely make it work. He would love nothing more than to ask her to be his wife, but he couldn't do it while she was in school. That wasn't fair to her, to have her give up her opportunities at 18 so that he could chase his? No. He wouldn't allow it. And he had such a strong faith in God, he knew that if they were meant to be together, that they would be, and they would have even more life experience under their belts to make it work. He would wait for her. Another option had never once crossed his mind, but he wanted to do it knowing she was free to become who she was meant to be, a photographer with a God-given talent who changed how people saw the world.

His eyes welled with tears and he quickly wiped them away with the sleeve of his shirt. His heart was racing. He planned this conversation for a time when he knew they would be home alone, and that was now. He didn't want to embarrass her and didn't want her to have to walk by his family when she left. He stood and turned his stereo on low, the silence already deafening. And then from downstairs, he heard her call his name.

Chapter Seventeen

Then

Sadie knocked lightly and opened the door to Mason's room, so excited to see him and compare their fall school schedules. Even though they had a rule of not being in either of their rooms alone, she knew this was a bit different. She would be sure to keep his door open, and they weren't just hanging out and lazing around, they were finally planning!

He had told her a couple of weeks ago that some new courses had opened up in his Business Administration program and that he was going to try and get into them, which would change his schedule for the fall. They made a plan to look at their calendars again when Sadie got back from her week-long summer road trip with Emily.

The road trip was a tradition Sadie and Emily started last year and intended to keep going. Emily's mom had finally given in to her begging and agreed that she was old enough to stay in Nova Scotia with her dad for the summer while her mom went to Mexico. Last year her and Sadie celebrated by taking a week to drive around Nova Scotia. They camped at different locations and hiked a bunch of scenic routes along the Cabot Trail in Cape Breton, blasting Stephen Curtis Chapman's 'The Great Adventure' so loud on the drive that they thought they would break Emily's car stereo. For years it had been their favorite song, and they still loved referring to everything new as 'A Great Adventure!'.

This year the girls had taken five days to drive all around Prince Edward Island, eating litres of ice cream and embracing the life of a tourist. Sadie had had so much fun but was excited to be back home and finally see her boyfriend, to share pictures from her trip and hear about how his week went.

She had her pencil case of pens and highlighters with her, excited to create new schedules for them, blocking out time for classes, his practices, time to study, hang out together- all the things that caused Mason to often and lovingly refer to her as his 'adorable little nerd'.

He was standing back to her, fiddling with his stereo, one of his mixed CD's had just started. Wearing a thin T-shirt and jeans, she noticed how strong he had become. His shoulders were broad and his arms muscular. Between watching his diet and playing so much hockey, he had dropped any baby fat he had left. They had been dating for just over three years and she still found him so hot, which was fun. She couldn't wait to marry him so that no one cared if the bedroom door was shut or not.

She dropped her pencil case and her sticky-tab filled U of T admissions catalogue on his bed and walked up behind him, wrapping her arms around him and squeezing, nuzzling her head into his back.

"Hey babe." She murmured, "I missed you so much."

She waited for him to turn around and wrap her in one of his amazing hugs, but he was feeling unnaturally stiff. He didn't reach for her hands in front of him, or turn his body to her at all. She gave it another couple of seconds.

"Babe?"

She could feel him take a deep breath and then he gradually turned, staying in the same spot, now looking down at her. She noticed immediately that under the bill of his hat his eyes were red and swollen, almost like he had been crying.

"Oh Mason!" She exclaimed, stepping back so she could see all of him better, then quickly stepping forward, bringing her hands to hold his face lightly. "What's wrong!?"

He didn't say anything, his chin quivering now. It looked like something was physically stopping him from being able to talk. He wiped at his eyes, as tears had begun to fall.

"Mason? Please. What's wrong? Is everyone ok? Where's your family? Your parents? Is everything ok with Jenny and Liam?"

He slowly nodded and brushed the back of his hands against his eyes again. Working to pull himself together, he knew he had to talk.

"We need to talk." was what he managed to get out.

"Sure babe. Let's sit down." An impending breakup was the absolute last thing on her mind. She was so worried about him, he was her other half. Whatever he needed, she would do it. They sat on his bed.

She waited, watching him with concern and allowed him to collect his thoughts. She placed her hand on his leg, slowly rubbing her fingers back and forth across his knee. He picked up her hand and placed it on the bed.

"Oh Sade." He was looking down, would not make eye contact with her.

"Oh Mase." She was trying to make him smile, but when he finally looked up at her, her smile fell. She felt the blood drain from her face and her heart suddenly palpitated. Her heart was slowing, not racing. She immediately recognized the look in his eyes, even though it was not one she had seen from him before. Guilt. The blood must be draining from her fingers as well, the ones he had just touched, they suddenly felt like icicles.

She stood. "What did you do?"

He looked at her, confused. "I didn't do anything."

"Who is she?"

"Who is who?"

"Whoever it is that is making you have that look on your face Mason!" She was yelling, pointing at him. She knew she was yelling and she didn't know why. This was not a normal reaction to someone's 'look' but her heart knew. It *knew*. Something was very wrong.

"You think I cheated on you?"

"I don't know what to think Mason! You aren't saying anything!"

He put his head down, hurt that that is where she immediately went, but also getting a glimpse into how this conversation was probably going to go. He needed to man up and just say it.

"Sadie, I want to break up."

As if a set of invisible hands had come up and pushed her from behind, she felt herself stumble forward.

Mason immediately stood and caught her, lowering her to the bed. The fight had fled from her, she lost her energy. Her head felt unusually heavy and she lowered it between her knees as the tears started and she began silently sobbing. She tried to keep it together. Her shoulders started to heave as her lungs sought air, she had lost control of her body.

"Sadie." He had his hand on her back now. He started to slowly rub it. She pulled away, not aggressively, but in soft desperation. She couldn't let him touch her. It made it hurt more.

"Sadie," he repeated.

She looked up at him and his breath stopped short. He would go on to remember that look for the next 15 years.

"Why? Did I do something wrong?" was all that she was able to get out.

He was panicked and wanted to explain quickly so that she could understand.

"I didn't cheat on you Sadie. I never have, and I never would. Ever. I love you too much for that."

A sad sound escaped her, one that relayed that she thought he was anything but funny.

"We need to break up Sadie because I'm moving away." His voice sounded urgent. He needed her to understand. "I'm not going to Ontario."

She processed what he was saying and her response was the same feeling as one would feel when realizing they had just woken up from a bad dream, and that it had just been that- a nightmare, not reality. Her boyfriend wasn't *actually* breaking up with her, he was just moving! She wiped her eyes and nose with the sleeve of her shirt. She was getting her energy back, her heart rate picked up. She turned to look at him, her eyes swollen. "Ok, so what! That doesn't mean we have to break up! We can get through anything Mason. We love each other! We tell each other every day."

"But this is different Sadie, we can't keep dating."

She was in problem solving mode now, as she began to catch her breath. "Well where are you moving to? I'll go too."

"British Columbia."

"Ok, so I'll come... Why is your family moving to BC?"

He paused, "It's not my family, it's just me."

She was confused. "Why are you moving to BC alone?"

"Because I got a full-time contract with the Bisons last week, Sade. I'm going to take my degree online, I'm going to play in the AHL."

Her heart filled with pride, but that pride was currently in an active battle with confusion and anger and sadness so she couldn't articulate it.

"I don't understand what that has to do with us? I'll go to school in BC."

"No Sadie, you have a full scholarship to U of T."

"Ok, so I'll apply for one in BC. Who cares where I go?" Her voice sounded different, nasally from crying.

When he didn't answer her, she sniffed again and added, "Why are you trying to stop me from being with you?"

"Because it'll be too hard." Mason replied. "I'll be busy. I'll be training and playing all the time. I won't have the time to sit with you while you study, or come visit you, or vice versa. I'll need to focus on hockey. You'll need to focus on school. You should be going to your dream school, and I should be doing this."

"So it doesn't really have anything to do with me and my scholarship." She stood. Sadness had made a comeback and her emotions were trying to keep up. "You want to be single.

You want to play in the NHL and you don't want me in your way."

"No Sadie." He stood, pleading for her to understand. He grabbed her hands, "It's not that. I just want you to do what you want and I want to do what I want, and for the next four years, at least, those things aren't the same thing."

"What are you even talking about Mason? I want to be with you! I love you! Can't you see that!?"

"Of course I can see that Sadie. It's not about that." Mason was panicking. He let go of her hands.

"What else could it possibly be about!? We're adults and are making life decisions, something, may I remind you, that we've been talking about doing together! Forever! And I am deciding that I want to be with you!"

He didn't know what else to say. He wanted her to be able to enjoy a full scholarship to her dream school, without his distance dragging her down.

Her mind was spinning. She knew he loved her. None of this made sense.

"Is this because we haven't slept together yet?"

He felt like he had been kicked in the stomach. Now it was his turn to sit. "W...What?"

It was starting to come together. Sadie couldn't believe she hadn't thought of it before. "You've been coming back and forth for 2 years now. I know there's hockey bunnies hanging around the rinks up there, they're down here too. Now you're going to an even bigger league with women who will want you, who will give you whatever you want. You don't want a girlfriend in school who is saving herself for marriage."

Mason's blood pressure was through the roof. He had never raised his voice at anyone in his life, but this took the cake. "I have NEVER thought that Sadie. I have NEVER pressured you, or made you feel like I wanted something more from you. We are BOTH saving ourselves for marriage. It has NOTHING to do with that."

But looking at him now, Sadie didn't buy it. He was becoming a full-grown man, he was gorgeous. He was the best hockey player this province had seen in decades, maybe ever. Nothing else made any sense to her. She loved Mason. She wanted to be with him. She offered to move schools for him. To move cities. She would follow him anywhere, be what he needed, but he didn't want her there. He wanted more. Something else. What else could that be?

"Ok Mason." The anger had left, the sadness, confusion, all side-stepping to let this train of desperation and embarrassment through. She was embarrassing herself. "Let me make sure I clearly understand this before I leave. I told you I love you. You told me you know that I mean it. I am willing to move with you to BC. I am willing to support you however I can. I want my degree, but I am willing to get it at a different school- Just so I can be close to where you are." She summoned the courage to hear the answer she dreaded was coming, "You know all of this, that I love you and I would go anywhere to be closer to where *you* are and your response is.. that you want to break up with me? That it's... over? Us? You and me... we're over?"

Mason sighed. What else could he say, the rest would just be semantics. "Yes, you're right. I want to break up."

Sadie just stared at him, her tears had subsided.

Mason continued, "If we're both still single when you're done school, then we can get back together."

"But maybe after four years one of us won't be single, is that right Mason?"

Now it was his turn to stare at her.

She rubbed the tears from her eyes and shaking her head, picked up her admissions book and pencil case from his bed. She gazed around his room, knowing it would be the last time she would ever be in it. She saw on his desk a framed photo of her favorite picture of the two of them, the ticket to their prom pinned to a dried out corsage attached to his bulletin board, his summer gym program pinned to the wall above his weight bench, his CD's that they had spent hours listening to together, his keys to the car she would never again sit in, the collages of framed memories that had been years in the making- gifts that she had spent hours perfecting. She headed to leave, the bedroom door still open, taunting her of everything that could have been.

She turned back to look at him. "Mason?"

He looked up, his eyes wet again, matching hers.

"Congratulations on your contract. Seriously. It's amazing. I know how hard you've worked for it. I know you'll do great.

"Thanks," he said, his voice cracking.

"And hey," she paused, making sure he could see how serious she was. "I don't know why, but you've ruined everything we ever had."

Chapter Eighteen

Now

Sadie rolled over from a restless sleep and habitually looked at her clock sitting on her nightstand- 5:30AM. She was rarely surprised by the time, her circadian rhythm an ever faithful companion, always waking her before the sun began its ascent over the horizon. While there were some days where she wished she could just sleep in, more often than not she was thankful that she woke early and had some quiet time to herself before her kids rose from their slumber and the demands of the day began.

Early Saturday mornings had become her favorite time of the week and knowing that while she'd soon get to spend the day with her children, right now she looked forward to that first sip of hot hazelnut flavored coffee and some quiet time with her thoughts and her journal.

Getting out of bed she noticed a few crumbs by her alarm, evidence reminding her that the night before she had finished the last of her mom's homemade cookies. She headed for the kitchen and lazily flipped on the coffee machine, thankful she had taken the time to prepare the pot the night before. She noticed one of her portfolios sitting on her kitchen table along with a stack of contracts her business manager Jeffrey had asked her to review. The contracts had already been reviewed by Jeffrey and were now covered in brightly colored sticky notes identifying where Sadie should focus her attention while reviewing.

Back when Sadie was in university and before she had kids, she worked six, sometimes seven days a week and hadn't thought twice about it. She rarely took a Saturday off. Monday through Saturday had been go-time and it had not only been good for Seaside Studios and her customers, but the creativity it required had energized her. The time flew and her business grew. During those years she lived for the hustle, knowing that once she had a family of her own and kids came along, they would become her priority, which as it turned out, is exactly what happened. Late in her pregnancy, she had made a conscious effort to slow down and transition her weekend tasks into her weekly schedule and with the help of a wonderful team, had been able to maintain mostly work-free weekends since her children were born. A blessing she acknowledged and was thankful for.

In the last few years, Sadie's early Saturday mornings had consisted of reading a novel, always in her pajamas while enjoying a hot drink- coffee, tea or lemon water, the choice depending on both the season and her mood.

After prompting from DivorceCare, she had recently begun journaling again. She had always loved to read and write outside whenever the weather allowed, though with a physical aversion to being cold, those mornings were rare. Still, there was something she loved about journaling in the fresh air, hearing the sounds of nature, and emptying her brain of everything circulating in it. It helped settle her heart and her mind.

Earlier in the week when she had made the commitment to begin journaling again, she had no idea that it would be so soon that she would be writing that she had talked to Mason again. She had been ruminating on her parking lot encounter with him all week, her feelings going back and forth between anticipation at the thought of more conversations with him, and regret when she thought about how things between them had ended- how her whole life could have been different if he had wanted her more than he had wanted hockey.

A nervous energy had permeated her week and she was itching to talk it all through with Scarlett and Emily. Scarlett was currently on vacation with her husband Peter and their daughters and she didn't want to interrupt that. She would fill her in when she got home. Scarlett lived in between her and her parents and having her and Peter and her nieces so close thrilled Sadie to no end.

Knowing Em had a busy week at work this week, she had also left her alone until yesterday when she couldn't take it anymore and had texted asking if they could grab dinner soon, giving her a quick flyover of what happened. Emily had enthusiastically agreed and they had plans tonight to go to their favorite seafood bar where she would fill her best friend in. Emily had always liked Mason, even after they broke up, which at times had really bothered Sadie. Why wouldn't her friend just bash him with her? But Emily's response was always the same 'I'm not going to dislike someone who I know loves you as much as I do, no matter what his stupid mouth says'.

With the kids still sleeping, Sadie grabbed the sweater and blanket that she kept by the back door, turned on the outside light, and stepped out onto her back wooden deck, sliding the patio door closed behind her. She took a seat in her oversized padded patio chair and breathed in the fresh air, wrapping the blanket around her. The mornings were getting cooler now and she knew that within the next few weeks she'd be moving this activity inside until late Spring.

Sadie had always invested in her journals, loving the feel of something hefty in her hands. She'd moved away from the key-locked journals she kept in high school and from brightly colored moleskin journals that she used in university. There was less room to write in those and the pages filled too quickly. She now wrote in leather bound journals that were good quality without being obnoxious, the texture and weight of them reminding her to take the time when writing, that her words didn't have to be rushed. She had always journaled the same way each week, covering what happened in her life the previous week and how she felt about it, writing about what she knew was coming up in her life and how she was feeling about that, and for the longest time had added in prayers she was praying, underlining them so that she could go back and see how God had answered her. She had left out that last part after her divorce, she felt that God had stopped answering her and she didn't need a reminder of it. It was, though, always interesting for her to scan back on previous weeks to see how the things she had been worried about had turned out. More often than not, she found that she had worried for naught and that continual weekly insight had helped her manage her emotions better than many other women her age.

Sadie noticed this morning as she grabbed her pen and looked for the next clean page, that she was getting close to the end of her journal and would have to pick a new one up the next time she was out. Once she filled a journal, she put it up on the top shelf of her closet. She didn't want to throw it out, but she never went back through them- she preferred to be moving forward. Reading about how she was feeling at different times in her past seemed counterintuitive.

She can only recall one time that she had felt pulled to go back and read her old journal entries, back when her kids were little and she had still been married. On a morning that started much like this one, going back and reading her own words on a different day had provoked such an immediate and intense reaction to the pain that she had been trying to mask that she had felt propelled to force a conversation with Nick, physically unable to stop herself. It was a conversation that turned into an argument, that turned into the end of their marriage. In the couple of years following, she had gone back to that morning so often, sometimes thankful for it, sometimes feeling so guilty it threatened to overtake her. With time had come perspective and now she leaned heavily towards gratitude for standing up for herself when she did.

Sadie stared now at the almost-filled journal in her lap. The sun was rising to her east, and the light of dawn began warmly illuminating the blank page in front of her. As she was about to put her pen to paper, she noted with amusement that the ends of her journals always seemed to coincide with life events big enough that the following journal would be themed differently from her last. A journal from junior high filled up the summer before high school, coinciding with when she began dating Mason. Another one the summer he broke up with her, as she was about to head to university. She had another two from her years in university, the first one covered her years as a new university student and all that entailed, filling up as she had met Nick and they had just begun dating. The second ending as she approached graduation and prepared to move back to Nova Scotia to begin married life. And on and on- being pregnant, having babies, babies turning into toddlers. All of the emotions from her divorce had been journaled including learning to be single again while being a mom at the same time, navigating the ensuing emotions of heartbreak, frustration with God, wherever He was. The expansion of her business and increasing business opportunities had been a thread through each of her journals no matter what was going on in her personal life.

She couldn't help but wonder as she flipped through the last few empty pages of this journal, what would occupy the next one. Dispersed through her life updates, this journal had held an underlying theme of a longing to know what her future held. She had some big decisions to make for Seaside Studio, but was that it? Was her life from here on out going to continue to revolve around her work, and Jacob and Tess? She loved being a mom but recognized her kids would eventually be grown and gone and, then what? She wrote last almost a full year ago. Back then she had been asking her journal all of her questions, and this morning as she looked up toward a beautiful purple pastel sky, she couldn't help but feel that nervous energy again wondering how this next journal might be different. The timing of this one ending the same week she ran into Mason seemed significant somehow. Was it merely a coincidence, or was it more than that?

She couldn't help but be filled with a sense of hope of what was to come and that was something she hadn't felt in a long, long time. She couldn't wait to talk to Emily.

Chapter Nineteen

Then

Sadie rolled over in bed, away from her husband toward the window that had been left slightly ajar the night before, a cool breeze now infiltrating the room. She saw that it was still dark outside, and closed her eyes, wishing she could go back to sleep. Readjusting her pillow, she pulled her heavy comforter up to her chin. Lying there she knew it was going to be another early morning, her body felt heavy and tired, but her mind had woken first and was ready to start the day. Knowing that trying to get back to sleep would be a futile effort, she pulled herself up out of bed and quietly found a sweater and her slippers, deciding to go do something productive rather than lie here in bed and let her mind work itself into a tailspin before the day even began.

She shuffled into the still dark kitchen, turning on the small light above the oven so she could get to work preparing a pot of coffee. She put her Michael Bublé CD into the CD player and turned it on low, his voice quietly breaking through the silence and setting the tone for the relaxing morning she'd hoped to have before Nick and the kids woke for the day. When her coffee was ready, she poured herself a cup and carried it over towards her chesterfield chair where she set it on the side table next to her well-worn bible, tucked in its protective forest green case. A blue Bic pen and a neon pink highlighter that someone had chewed the cap on, laid next to the case. On top of her bible sat her almost filled journal and a new unopened one, waiting to be broken in. She turned on the floor lamp which sat behind her chair and with the smell of coffee in the air, Michael crooning from the corner and the soft lighting, she looked forward to some time alone.

Settled deep into her living room chair, she pulled down the blanket that was behind her folded on the chair and covered her lap. With the coffee cup warming her hands, she looked out of the oversized picture window to see the silhouettes of the maple, spruce and elm trees that lined their driveway. They were dark and hidden now but ready and waiting to show off their needles and bright leaves once the sun rose.

It was Easter Monday, and she didn't have to work today. Though it wasn't a statutory holiday in Nova Scotia, she had told her team to take the day off. She needed a down day and figured they did as well. She was really hoping the kids would sleep in this morning after the festivities from yesterday. They were five now and everything about the holidays was exciting to them. She smiled to herself as she stared out of the window, remembering Jacob and Tess running up and down the driveway the day before looking for Easter eggs that she and Nick had spent an hour hiding, and that they had in turn found in 15 minutes. The kids had been so excited to hunt for eggs after church. When they took off together, Tess had still been in her Easter dress and Jacob in his new ninja turtle jogging pants and matching sweater, both wearing their little yellow rubber boots. Jacob had pulled Tess along the driveway and across the yard, pointing out eggs to her that he had seen first, making sure they each collected some.

Her and Nick had laughed watching them squeal in excitement, and he had put his arm around her shoulder as they watched the kids run around. She remembered feeling surprised at the touch, and had leaned into it, trying not to say or do anything that would make him move his arm. When they were all found, Nick went inside to take a nap and she and the kids had spent the afternoon outside playing with the bubbles and sidewalk chalk that had been in their Easter baskets, a pile of plastic Easter Eggs sitting next to them. They only came back into the house when it was time to get cleaned up to get ready to go to her parents for supper.

It had been a good day with Nick, she thought now, taking a sip of her coffee. As she silently thanked God for that, her heavy heart wasn't matching her words. She stopped then and wondered if other women categorized days with their husbands like that, in good days and not very good days. Sadie spent a lot of time talking to God about her marriage. It was absolutely one of the hardest things in her life and the emotions it provoked consumed her thoughts on most days. She continued to trust and pray that something would change, but it was wearing her down. She had asked Nick a few months ago on a particularly hard day, after a particularly hard fight, if he'd consider going to couples counselling with her and he had no interest, saying he didn't need a stranger in their business.

The crux of their problem, she knew, was that she didn't know how to make him happy. They had met when they were both attending the University of Toronto. She had been in her second year studying visual design, and he was in his fourth, studying economics. They had sat next to each other in a cross-over business strategy course and he had asked her to go out on a date with him immediately after that first class.

Prior to him asking, she had been on a few dates since arriving in Toronto, with guys that her roommate and new friends had set her up with. And while they were all nice guys, there were no sparks. And after Mason, Sadie knew the importance of sparks.

Nick had been different than the guys her friends had been setting her up with. He was a couple of years older than her and had enjoyed talking business. He had made a comment in that first class they had together that had made her think differently about the marketing aspect of her own business. She was intrigued, and while they had no mutual friends, he was handsome in a nerdy sort of way, and she remembered feeling flattered when he asked her out. She was missing home, missing her family, and looked forward to talking to someone who could distract her- not only from her homesickness, but from hearing about how awesome Mason was playing in the AHL, because of course her family couldn't help but update her every time he broke a new record.

She knew her parents had held out hope that they would get back together, but even if she had wanted that too, she hadn't heard from Mason at all that first year. She had been offered a paid internship in Toronto her summer between first and second year and she had decided to take it. Not only was it good for her professional development, but it also meant she didn't have to risk running into Mason when they were both at home in Nova Scotia for the summer, a position she wasn't ready to put her heart in.

Nick had come along at a time when she was trying to move forward, and she had taken his interest in her as a sign that everything would be ok, that fresh starts were in fact possible.

As Sadie grabbed her pen and flipped open her journal to find the next empty page, she thought about how her parents would react if they knew now how unhappy she was, how fractured her relationship with Nick had become.

When the arguments between her and Nick had first started, Sadie had been too embarrassed to say anything to her mom. Her mom had, after all, been vocal with Sadie in her concerns when she brought Nick home to Nova Scotia for the first time. At the time, Sadie wouldn't hear any of it. At Caroline's insistence, and much to Stephen's dismay, Stephen had taken Nick for a drive on a tour of Darlings so Caroline could talk privately with Sadie. They had ended up in such a big fight that they had both ended up crying. Sadie had accused her mom of not loving her as much as she loved Mason, of only caring about him and that no matter who she brought home, if it wasn't Mason, she knew she wouldn't have her approval- and it wasn't fair, she had screamed, because Mason didn't want *her*. Caroline couldn't say anything right, and Sadie had told Nick the following morning that they had to fly back to Toronto earlier than expected as she had work to do. He had been completely unaware of her parents' reservations. Her mom and Sadie had eventually worked it out, with Caroline acknowledging that Sadie was an adult and she could make her own decisions, adding that she wouldn't share her thoughts about Nick with Sadie again unless she was asked to. While Sadie appreciated it at the time, even she knew deep down, that that was a compromise that didn't feel right.

Seven years and two children later, just the thought of talking to her parents about how she was feeling, to risk disappointing them, it made her stomach physically hurt. She did her best to cover her unhappiness whenever she could, which honestly wasn't that hard given how busy everyone was. When she was with her parents they had so much to talk about, updates on her parents lives, on Scarlett's life, Seaside Studio, and filling her parents in on the kids, monopolized most of their conversations.

Only Scarlett and Emily had any idea that things weren't as great as she'd tried to make them out to be, and that was only because Nick made more snide comments around them than he did when her parents were around, which always caused Emily and Scarlett to check for Sadie's reaction. Sometimes she was able to hide it, other times not.

Now, Sadie began writing and started with the things she was thankful for. They had a good Easter. Jacob and Tess were happy and healthy, they were in grade primary this year and had adjusted well to the school routine. Things were going good at work- she had just hired a new business manager, Jeffery, whom she loved and had come highly recommended, and she had other things to be excited for as well. Scarlett and Peter had announced last night at their family dinner that she was pregnant. Jacob had teed up the announcement perfectly by randomly asking her in between dinner and dessert why he and Tess couldn't have cousins like the other kids at school did. Sadie had tried to shush Jacob, knowing Scarlett wanted kids more than anything, and then Scarlett had surprised them all by sharing with Jacob that he would in fact be getting a cousin, in approximately five months. Her and her mom had both jumped from the table screaming. Her dad laughed but remained stoic, and Peter, well he looked like he was going to be the proudest dad that had ever existed. She was so excited to become an aunt and for Jacob and Tess to be getting a cousin. Nick didn't have siblings so the pressure had fallen to Aunt Scarlett and Uncle Pete to help make it happen.

Giving her hand a rest, she looked up and noticed the two multi colored wicker Easter baskets sitting on the couch, tipped over and empty except for the colored paper straw covering the bottom of the baskets which now held only a few brightly colored foil wrappers that had been discarded haphazardly once the chocolate inside was discovered.

Despite everything she had to be thankful for, her heart was still heavy, and she had been writing for the last 20 minutes, pleading with God again to please help her figure out how to be happy, how to make her marriage work. She was about to close the journal, she had filled the last page, but when she went to reach for her new journal so she could keep writing, pictures of her children on the wall across from her caught her eye.

Chapter Twenty

Then

Setting down her journal, she took in her son and daughter beaming at her from their pre-school pictures that were taken last Spring, just before their fifth birthday. Jacob had been wearing a Blue Jays t-shirt that day, the bright blue from his shirt popping against the white of his little pre-school gown, the graduation cap covering his tiny cow lick, a toothy grin on display as he smiled for the camera. In her picture, Tess had two long braids, her bangs cut straight and her light brown hair falling just above her eyebrows. Her dimple popped through her wide smile. She was struck then by their baby teeth and their tiny faces, and how happy they both looked.

The CD switched songs then, another slow ballad playing from her kitchen, but instead of feeling calm as she had moments before, her heart started racing and she wasn't sure what had triggered the change. She had put those pictures in their frames, she had hung them up herself and had walked by them hundreds of times, but she had never had a reaction to them like she had as she stared at them this morning. It was like she was seeing them for the first time- and a flood of everything that she wanted for them washed over her.

She knew she would give up anything, do absolutely anything in the world to keep them safe and happy. A quick glance again at Tess's picture and she was reminded of a picture she had seen in a photo album at her parents' house not long ago. The album had been the kind where printed pictures were stuck to white rippled self-adhesive pages covered in plastic. She had been on her parents' couch and was flipping through pages, Jacob on her lap, when she had come across her own little pre-school face from over 20 years earlier beaming up at her. She had had a great childhood, and though the picture should have made her smile, it had made her sad, and she hadn't been able to pinpoint why. She had quickly turned the page, shaking off her unsettled feeling.

Emotion rose in her throat now, pushing tears to the surface, and she quickly looked away from the pictures toward her window. The pressure in her chest was almost unbearable as she sat in her adult chair in her adult house, overlooking her adult yard with her adult trees, listening to her adult music, and thought of the little girl she used to be.

She didn't pick up her new journal and begin writing as she had planned. She had finished the last one with the news of Scarlett's pregnancy and prayers for help with her marriage. She sat there staring at her bible and felt pulled to go back through the journal that she had just finished, before moving onto a new one, something she rarely did. She opened the first page of the book and noticed the date of the entry was just over a year prior. She always underlined her prayers and as she began flipping through the journal and reading just her prayers, she noticed the increasing desperation in her pleas for God to please help her. Going back to the beginning again, she skimmed through some of the first pages, reading words that she had forgotten she'd written, suddenly reading them as if they were words written by someone else. Her stomach turned and she was left with a deep guttural sadness for this woman. She read page after page. She hadn't realized that she was crying until she saw the ink she was reading starting to run, her tears like a loose faucet, falling steadily onto the pages. Her sadness turned to desperation and again she found herself questioning God, asking him how it was that she was here, in this position. She had only ever wanted to make Him happy, to do what she thought He wanted from her, and it hadn't mattered. Had it ever mattered? Why had He forgotten about her?

She was so overwhelmed at what she had been reading, that she didn't hear Nick come down the hall until he grunted a 'hey' and flicked on all the kitchen lights, pulling her from her prayer. He walked through the now-bright kitchen and turned off her music, no thought that maybe his wife had been enjoying the quiet music and soft lighting. He started rummaging around the kitchen, opening and closing cupboards, sighing and slamming the dishwasher door as he looked for a specific mug that he couldn't seem to find. She pulled up the bottom of her tank top from under her sweater, quickly wiping her tears. Nick hated it when she cried, had told her early in their marriage that it was juvenile and not to come talk to him until she could pull herself together.

He had been about to ask her where his mug was, when he looked over and saw that she had been crying. "Jesus Christ, Sadie. It's 6AM. What's wrong already?"

She felt herself flinch. She hated it when he used the Lord's name in vain. As a teenager she had listened to a really impactful sermon on how the language that we use matters. The first time she had heard one of the kids say 'Oh My God' when they were playing she had knelt down and told them kindly that they weren't in trouble but that they shouldn't say that- they could say 'Oh My Gosh, or Oh My Goodness' instead, 'We should only say God when we're talking to God, or about God, ok?' Sadie had gently guided them, 'That's what the bible says'. She didn't know Nick had been standing behind her until she heard him scoff and told her to get a grip, that they were just kids.

Sadie didn't know what had suddenly come over her. Maybe it was the combination of seeing her children's pictures on the walls and reading that desperately sad journal, but her heart headed down a path she rarely dared step. The sudden bright light in the kitchen and Nick's frustration seemed to have illuminated it.

"I'm not happy." She was surprised to hear herself say.

"No kidding." he replied, turning back to the kitchen.

"Nick, I'm serious. We need to talk about it." She was finding her voice, but she didn't get out of her chair. She had been hoping he'd come sit down with her. "I'm really not happy and I don't think you are either."

He laughed and she instantly cringed. She hated his fake laugh the most. He didn't answer her, but he had slowed his movements, no longer looking for anything. He slowly turned and stared at her, questioning with his eyes if she was serious.

She had never remembered her parents having arguments before, and so had never dared ask her mom how to handle them. At that point in her life, she knew her parents had no idea what she had been going through and would have been heartbroken to hear. Sadie didn't like to compare her relationship to others, but she knew her dad would never talk to her mom the way Nick talked to her. She knew that as fiercely as she suddenly knew how wrong this all was.

"What?" she asked, "Am I wrong?"

"No Sadie, you're not wrong." He shook his head and smirked as if this was a big joke.

She knew that this conversation wasn't going to go as she'd hoped and began praying through her panic. *God help me. God help me. God help me.*

"Since when do you care if I'm happy?" he added then.

"What do you mean? Of course I care."

"No, you don't. You only care about yourself."

"How can you say that!?" She said, "I've been trying to make you happy for years Nick! I never know how to do it. Sometimes it seems like you're happy, and then all of a sudden it's like you remember you're married and you get so mad again."

"Because I never wanted to marry you!" he boomed at her.

She recoiled as if she'd been slapped. Her heart was racing again and her eyes began burning, she suddenly felt light headed. She gripped both sides of her chair to keep her grounded. As much as she had thought that was the case, she couldn't believe he had just said it.

"Nick..." She caught the sight of the two little smiling faces in their pre-school pictures and she didn't have the strength to hold anything in. She began sobbing and pulled up her knees to her chest so she could rest her head in them.

"I'm sorry Sadie, but it's true." He wasn't even angry now, he had lowered his voice and was talking to her in his matter-of-fact tone, as if they were talking about someone else, as if he hadn't just picked up her heart and slammed it against a wall. He crossed his arms over his chest and leaned back against their kitchen island. "And if we're suddenly being so honest, I think you knew that. And that's what makes me so mad. I've been mad for years. I think I've done a pretty good job of pretending to want to be here."

He had to pretend to want to be married to her? To be a family with her and Jacob and Tess? Despite all her personal reservations, she had offered to move their family to Ontario before, hoping that being in his home province would bring him some peace, but he had never wanted that. He had wanted to keep Ontario as a travel destination, not a home base.

"Leave then!" The racing of her heart had ignited a fire that burst out of her, she stood, yelling now. She hated yelling but there was no way she could control it. Something else had taken over her body, all sense of control gone. "Why are you still here then? I don't need you! Just go!" She was pointing to the door.

"If I thought I could Sadie, I would." He was still not yelling, he was calm and was watching her closely.

"Why can't you Nick?" She didn't know where this was coming from. She had been trying for years to keep them together, but suddenly she meant everything she was saying. "Go! Just go back to Ontario! I'll keep the kids! You don't want us anyway. I have a good job, I have family here, I can make it. I don't need you!" She was so mad, "God, I don't even want you!"

And it was as if she had finally given him the permission to do something he had been longing to do for years. His shoulders dropped and he exhaled. Walking over to her, he wrapped his arms around her. She was shaking in his arms. She tried to push him away but he held her close until her crying ceased and she was able to breath in a slower, steady rhythm. He held her back and looked at her then, looked her in the eyes. She was focused on the rims of his glasses, waiting to hear him apologize for saying what he had just said. That's how all of their arguments went. A blow up and an apology. Though he had never told her before that he didn't want to marry her, she waited to hear that he was sorry, that of course he loved her, of course he wanted to be married to her. They would figure it out like they always did.

"Do you mean it?" he asked then, gently.

"Do I mean what?" She had a dull thud growing behind her eyes, the light from the kitchen felt blinding.

"Do you think that we could do that? Separate? I could go back to Ontario and you could stay here? I'll pay you whatever I'm supposed to, but Sadie, you're right, I know we aren't happy."

"Sure Nick. If that's what you want." She felt the fight leave her body, resigned that they were going to have to play this game.

"Ok," he said then, "Ok."

With that, he turned and walked back towards their bedroom and she heard the door shut. A few seconds later he was on his cellphone talking to who knows who. She walked down the hall and pushed open the door while he was mid-sentence, the phone to his ear.

"Who are you talking to?!" She was yelling again, "Who could you possibly be talking to!?"

"My Mom." And then to the phone, "Yeah, that's Sadie. I'll call you back."

Sadie knew that from the other end of the line, she probably sounded like a crazy woman. How had she gone from a quiet morning thanking God for Easter and the trees, to screaming at her husband in their bedroom, the possibility of a separation mounting over her.

"I'm going to go back to Ontario." he said then. "I'll make a reservation for a flight and head out as soon as I can."

"Just like that? And what am I supposed to tell the kids?" She knew they'd be up any moment now, if her yelling hadn't woken them already.

"I'll talk to them."

His calmness was increasing her frustration and she was suddenly panicked, thinking about Jacob and Tess and how they'd react to all of this.

"Nick, wait, I'm sorry. I'm really sorry. I shouldn't have said that. I shouldn't have said anything" She was crying now, again.

"No," he quickly shook his head. He seemed concerned that she might change her mind and make this more difficult for him. "You were right Sadie. You just had the nerve to say something when I didn't.

Of course I love Jacob and Tess, but Sadie, I don't want to be married. I don't like anything about it. I knew it was important to you when we were younger so I did it for you, but coming home every day to the same house, the same routine, the same everything... I.... I hate it. I feel like a caged animal."

"You... only got married because I wanted to?"

"Yes. And like I said earlier, I think you know that."

She watched him, the hope in his eyes now obvious enough that it almost knocked her over.

"Alright. Well. Don't let me keep you." She got up and headed back to the living room.

Within a few hours, Nick, who was Branch Manager of a bank in Darlings, had called his boss's cell phone and told her that he was unexpectedly moving to Ontario and that if she was willing to post him to a position in the Toronto area, he would love to transfer, but that he 'unfortunately' had to leave his job in Darlings. That call was either followed by, or preceded by, a call to the airport where he booked a flight for Toronto leaving later that night.

He rolled his suitcase to the front door just before lunch. He had a three-hour drive to Halifax to make, and wanted to be sure he was at the airport early. Sadie watched everything that was happening around her in awe, like she was taking part in a movie but didn't know the script, just knew she was in the way of the other actors.

He gave the kids a kiss on the head and said he would see them soon, but that 'daddy had a plane to catch'. He turned as he lifted his suitcase over the door's threshold, letting Sadie know he would be in touch.

What was this? A job interview?

"When?" She had asked.

"I'll call soon."

And that, had been that. She watched him back out of the driveway and drive away, as the kids pulled on her pant leg asking again what was for lunch.

She made her way to the cupboard and pulled out two plastic plates, one pink and one blue, the small rims on the plate ready to hold anything that might overflow. She grabbed a box of crackers and poured some on each plate, putting the box back and then moving to the fridge on autopilot where she pulled out two apples and a cucumber. She began cutting up the food, barely hearing the television in her room turn on, or her kids giggling and play-fighting on her bed as the theme song for their favorite cartoon started.

As Sadie sliced the cucumber for her kids, placing them on their plates, she thought that Nick just must really need a break, wondering when he would call and say this was all a big mistake.

That day she had no way of knowing that it was not just a break that Nick needed.

She didn't know then that he would never again be her first call.

She didn't know then that they had made love for the last time, or that they had shared their last ever kiss.

She didn't know then that he would immediately get a great job in Toronto's Financial District, a huge promotion in fact, and that for the rest of his life, he would only see his kids an average of twice a year, the week after Christmas and for a week in the summer.

She didn't know then that his parents supported his return and would do anything to help their only son stay closer to them, having always thought that he had been too young to have kids and could have done better than a small-town girl from Nova Scotia.

She didn't know then that what started as a trial separation would turn into divorce papers appearing in her mailbox 10 months later.

She didn't know then that a time would come where weeks would go by and he wouldn't cross her mind, that their relationship would deteriorate to a point where when she saw him she felt nothing at all- no anger, no sadness, no love, only an occasional gratefulness that because of their relationship she had Jacob and Tess in her life.

Sadie didn't know then that it wouldn't be until Tess was 18 and found one of her mother's old journals hidden in the top of her closet, that Tess would read about the emotional abuse her mother had quietly endured, realizing with horror that her mom had never said anything to defend herself from Tess's careless remarks. Sadie would find her daughter on her bedroom floor, journal open, and would hold Tess while she sobbed, their relationship forever changed.

She didn't know then her relationship with Tess would become the strongest one she would ever have.

Nick didn't know then that despite how much money he sent them, or how many visits he made, that when his kids got older, they would lose any respect they had ever had for him.

He didn't know that they would refer to him as Saint Nick in the winter- the man who came to make a quick appearance and deliver gifts, and as Uncle Nick in the summer, the man who knew nothing about their real lives but wanted to make sure they had fun whenever they were together.

For now, as Sadie took great care in arranging the sliced cucumber and apples on the colored plastic plates, she found herself praying again, asking God to forgive her for her outburst that morning and begging him to please bring her husband back to her so they could find a way to work things out.

Chapter Twenty One

Now

The Sandbar was a locally cherished Seafood Bar and Restaurant that sat on Darlings' scenic coastline. Guests could sit inside and enjoy ocean themed decor and listen to live music, or on warmer days, could be served their meal and drinks outside and take in the utterly impressive Atlantic Ocean, where the breeze carried faint whiffs of algae and seaweed. While The Sandbar had become a hot spot for tourists and listed annually in various 'Must-Experience' lists, it was a treasure to locals and the host of many a family celebration. The waiters and waitresses were both young and old, and whether your server had grey hair or looked like they were still in high school, they were loud, fun and always happy to have you there.

Emily and Sadie had reserved a booth in the corner, where they didn't have to yell to hear each other, but could also enjoy the band, which tonight was made up of two young brothers from down shore who were playing a mix of Cape Breton and Celtic jigs. They had high energy and from Sadie's seat, she could watch the youngest master his fiddle while somehow also able to laugh and sing with his brother. She recognized some of the music they played but as much as she would have loved to sing along, she didn't have a musical bone in her body- zero rhythm she had been told by more than one exasperated music teacher. Alas, her musical fate had become to simply take it all in and enjoy the talent of others. To the amusement of many, her lack of rhythm had never stopped her from occasionally pulling out some impressive shoulder heavy dance moves.

"It's so funny," she said to Emily now, her volume slightly louder than her regular speaking voice, "People are coming in looking tired and cranky and then boom! Within 10 seconds I can see their feet start to tap."

Emily laughed, "I know! I love it!"

Within a few minutes, Adelle, the Manger of The Sandbar, had come to take their order. In her late 50's now, she had known both girls since they were young and no matter how often she saw them, she told them it had been 'far too long' and how wonderful it was to see them. Whether she said that to everyone or not, the girls did not know, but they ate it up and made small talk with Adelle as they finalized their orders. A seafood-topped garden salad for Sadie and a large plate of fish and chips, extra ketchup, extra vinegar, for Emily. They each ordered the night's drink special, an Ocean Blue Breeze Bomb, and settled in knowing they'd enjoy their evening together.

"I don't know how you eat like that and still keep that figure," Sadie commented now that Adelle had left, "I wouldn't be able to get in and out of the booth if I ate like you did."

Emily laughed again, "Genes, baby! Why do you think I'm such a devout Christian? I need to keep Jesus on my side so he doesn't take them away. I need fries and vinegar, in large quantities, for life."

"Ha! I don't think that's how it works."

"No, you're right. I guess it could also be the 5AM gym workouts," she chuckled. Then after a beat, "Ok. Tell me everything."

Sadie took a deep breath.

When Sadie left for the University of Toronto after high school, Emily stayed in Darlings Lake and went to the local Community College to study business. John Gray had hired Emily before she had even graduated with her diploma. He and Judy had gotten to know her through her close friendship with Mason and Sadie, and they had always enjoyed her positivity and sense of humor. When Judy heard that Emily's plans after high school were to stay close to home, she had encouraged John to reach out to her, feeling she could be beneficial for the company.

Knowing the Gray's as she did, Emily accepted John's job offer to be an office assistant following her graduation. She was tasked with keeping John's contacts, phone calls and messages organized, ensuring he called people back in a timely manner, and that he never forgot important meetings, a tendency that he had before she had come along. Within her first year, John realized she was being underutilized as an office assistant and could be used in a number of different areas. She was eager and excited about any opportunity given to her to continue to learn and grow. She was genuinely appreciative of being corrected and coached as she took on new tasks, and John was so impressed with her that he had asked her to become his Business Manager, a position she eagerly accepted. Getting a taste of international business and wanting to continue to grow professionally, Emily went back to school.

There was a time, when Sadie had first moved back to Darlings after her time in Toronto, that she hardly saw Emily at all. Emily had been working at Gray's Gear through the day, and her evenings and weekends were spent studying Human Resources and the Law, graduating with degrees in both. John began transitioning even more duties to her, including the hiring of staff, negotiating contracts, and plant operations. When she confided in him over a coffee and a honey cruller that she loved learning about the fishing industry, but that she didn't feel like she was becoming really good at just one aspect of it, he told her to take her choice of what she wanted to focus on- she could have it. She chose both human resources and contract management, overseeing human resources fulfilled her vehement desire to make sure staff were treated well, whereas contract management kept her involved and active in high-level business meetings.

She travelled internationally for the company often now and had developed into an aggressive negotiator who held a well-deserved reputation with buyers and their CEO's of being tough but always fair. She wasn't a pushover. She knew the products John had, and how much money their partners would go on to save, or make, once they arrived at a deal. Emily had made John millions above what he would have dared negotiate on his own, and while she never wanted a title more than Business Manager, everyone, especially John, knew she was much more than that, her title not clearly reflective of the value she added, which was fine by her.

"Before *I* start," Sadie said, "*Please* tell me how it got by you that Mason was back in town? Why didn't you tell me?"

Emily leaned in wide eyed, "I swear to you Sade, I had NO idea. I think he's only been home for a week or so? I finally had some time to talk to John today, we were meeting about other things and I told him I had heard Mason was back in town. He said that was the other thing he wanted to meet with me about and he let me know that he hired Mason as the VP of Operations. From what I understand he'll be based in Darlings, but like me, will travel when he needs to. Seriously, thank goodness though. I'm exhausted, and the fishing season hasn't even started yet... he could really help."

"Well, that's good I guess." Sadie looked up from the napkin she had been twisting in her lap. "Emily, seeing him again.... I can't even explain it."

When Mason had broken up with Sadie all those years ago, Emily had been almost as upset as Sadie was. She hated seeing her friend so broken and had gone to see Mason herself to try and figure out what was going on. Mason had said the same thing to her that he had said to Sadie, that the 'timing wasn't right', but Emily could immediately see that there was more to it than that. He looked nearly as upset as she had been. Looking at him then she had decided that she was going to stay out of it. She loved them both and trusted that God would help them figure it out. She never in a million years thought it would take this long.

"Tell me about it!"

"There isn't much to tell. He came out of the rink with Jacob's hockey bag on this shoulder."

"Wait, what?"

"Yes! And then I almost fainted."

Emily laughed. "I'm sorry, it's not funny. But like, how did he look?"

"So hot Em. I can't even."

They both started giggling then, just as Adelle came over with their drinks over her shoulder.

"Here you go ladies."

"Thanks Adelle." They both said in unison.

Emily picked up her drink just as the brothers put down their instruments, they'd be able to talk quietly for a bit while the boys took their break.

"Really though, how are you?" Emily looked at her friend. "You've been on my mind so much lately. How is DivorceCare going?"

"Good actually," Sadie replied, taking a sip of her drink as well. "Really good actually." She set down her glass. "It's been helpful. I'm glad I'm going. Can I ask you why you really wanted me to go so bad? I mean, I'm glad I'm there, but, what was it?"

Emily thought for a second before she responded. "And I can be honest?"

"Always."

"I already told you I missed you, how happy you used to be, but it's even more than that. I... Well.... I think you need to try to move on. I don't want to see 'Nick'..." Sadie laughed, despite herself. Emily had been literally air-quoting Nick's name since he left. She said that it would be inappropriate to use the term she wanted to, so she would instead settle for 'Nick' in air-quotes, an indication that that was not her pre-ferred handle for him, "ruin men for you." She continued, "I know that you loved him and that the breakup was hard, but *Sadie*, there are good men out there. Men who will treat you like the queen that you are, and I don't want to see you grow up to find your kids are grown and gone and you're living with three cats and living to watch 'Name that Price', slurping a bowl of soup."

Sadie almost spit the drink out of her mouth, "The Price is Right?"

"Yeah, whatever... You deserve more than that."

"I can't date again."

"Says who?"

"Says me. Says, I don't know... God!"

"Girl. What are you talking about. He doesn't say that."

"He says divorce is a sin."

"Yes, he doesn't want us divorced, and you know exactly why. Because it's a miserable experience, and it's hard on everyone involved, well, unless you're 'Nick', but Sadie, that doesn't mean that because you went through that, that he doesn't want you to ever be happy again, that he doesn't want you to be able to move on."

Sadie hadn't wanted to think about it too much. After she had finished reeling from Nick leaving, her energy had gone into trying to make sure the kids were ok, her left over energy went into Seaside Studios. She hadn't thought about wanting to start anything with anyone else. She had wanted to... what? Wallow?

"Em." Sadie's eyes suddenly filled with tears, "Don't you think I want to be happy? I hate him." She leaned in, "I hate how he left us, I hate how Jacob gets ready for a game hoping that his dad is going to show up to watch. I hate that Tess asks me all the time what dad is up to. I hate all of it. I'm tired. And I forget what it feels like to not be tired." She looked down, squeezing her eyes so the tears would stop.

"Sadie," Emily reached across the table and held out both of her hands, which Sadie took. "It's going to be ok. I promise you. God promises you. He knows the plans he has for you Sadie, plans to give you hope. A future. A future that is more than feeling like this. THAT is why I wanted you to go to the divorce group, so that you could be reminded of that."

Sadie gave her friend a soft smile, "I want to believe that."

"Believe it! You are one of the best people I know. You are fun, and funny, and you are loyal. To a fault. You love so big and you wear all of those emotions on your sleeve. I love that about you." She stopped.

"Sadie, look at me."

Sadie looked up.

"Will you do something for me?"

She had never been able to say no to Emily. "Yes."

"I want you to start praying again. Really praying like you did when you were younger, like you did when you were married and wanted help, like you have your whole life. Keep going to these meetings, find a counsellor that can help you move forward- I can give you some good names, and pray that God shows you what he wants for you, for the kids. He'll know that I told you to do it, but he'll listen to you anyway." She smirked. "Ok?"

"Ok."

"Really?"

"Yes, I'll pray."

"And keep going to meetings?"

"Yes. There's only a couple left."

"And find a counsellor?"

"Yes."

"Wonderful!" Emily exclaimed then, letting go of her hands. "Now, how hard was that? You big baby."

Sadie laughed again and grabbed her drink, taking a sip. She looked over towards the door and saw the youngest of the brothers pick up his fiddle.

Emily turned to look behind her, "Not him, he's like fourteen."

Sadie choked mid swallow and spit out her drink, blue liquid landing in a splatter on the front of Emily's beautiful white, probably very expensive, silk shirt.

"Serves you right." Sadie said, wiping the table in front of her, once again silently thanking God for Emily and her unwavering friendship.

Chapter Twenty Two

Now

Caroline and Stephen spent the night at Sadie's Saturday night. Caroline didn't want Emily and Sadie to feel rushed on their night out, and they would have been back to Sadie's in the morning anyway to pick the kids up for church, it had just made more sense for them to stay.

Walking down the hall the next morning, Caroline had been surprised to find Sadie up and dressed and applying mascara in the bathroom mirror.

"It just feels like it's time to go back to church," Sadie had responded to her mother's surprised look.

"I agree," her mom said. She had been asleep when Sadie got home and they hadn't had a chance to catch up on how her evening had gone.

"Did you have a nice night?"

"Yes. Thank you so much for staying." She turned and gave her mom a quick kiss on the cheek. "It was nice to spend a few hours together."

Caroline watched her daughter turn and finish applying her makeup. Sadie had stayed petite in stature but had only ever become more beautiful with age. For the first time in years, Caroline could see glimpses of the girl she used to be. A little lighter, a little more hopeful.

"We have some time for a coffee before church. Want me to make you one? I think your father is down there already."

"Yes! That would be great." Sadie hadn't gotten into the house until after midnight, her stomach sore from laughing, the beginning of a new plan taking shape in her heart.

Downstairs, Stephen was at the table perusing the Sunday newspaper and drinking a to-go cup of coffee. He had left the house early to go pick up the paper at the closest convenience store, disappointed that Sadie hadn't listened when he told her she should subscribe to a paper delivery like he and Caroline had. Gleaning news from internet sources, Stephen believed, was the equivalent to asking an inmate what they thought of the justice system, the response skewed based on their experience. He preferred his news come from an editor accountable to stick to the facts, he didn't need someone's opinion on what happened, he just wanted to know what happened, so the newspaper it was. He lowered the paper briefly to lift his head and kiss his wife as he felt her come up beside him. He could hear the kids upstairs and he couldn't imagine a better Sunday morning than spending it here.

Sadie came downstairs to find her parents at her kitchen table, a hot cup of coffee sitting between them that had her name all over it. She heard her dad try to cover his surprised cough from seeing her up and she leaned down and kissed him on the top of the head.

"Morning to you too Dad." She smiled, and settled in between them, feeling like a kid again, but in the best way.

"So," her mother started, "How's Emily?"

"Good. Really good, actually. Busy at work, she just got back from France! John has her everywhere."

"Wow. That's amazing. I know John and Judy really like her. The four of us had dinner last week, it's important for all of us to prioritize friendship. I'm glad you went out." Caroline responded.

"Can I ask you something mom?" Sadie asked, leaning back in her chair. Her legs were crossed and she felt relaxed. Her hands were wrapped around her cup, seizing the warmth. "I should have asked you a long time ago, but I never thought of it until this week. And now I feel bad that I never asked you before."

"Of course... I'm so curious."

"I know everything's fine now, but what happened after Mason and I broke up? I mean, with you guys, and Judy and John? Did you guys just keep hanging out? Thinking back, I left for Toronto almost right away and I was so caught up in my own feelings, that I never really asked how all of it had affected you."

Sadie saw her dad glance up from his paper and lift his eyebrows towards her mom. From across the table he nodded, like... 'go ahead, tell her'.

"Oh Sadie, we don't need to get into all that." Caroline started, "It's been so long now. What has it been? 15 years?"

"Fourteen."

"Exactly," she was about to change the topic, but something told her that this might be important for Sadie. "Well...that night you came home crying, I spent the whole night with you, I don't know if you remember. I just laid next to you and rubbed your back. You didn't want to talk about anything, but didn't want me to leave either. I didn't know if you guys had just gotten into a fight, or if it was more than that. I didn't even think about reaching out to Judy, but the next day, when you were able to tell me that he had broken up with you and that it was over, I did reach out to her that night. I was upset."

Stephen coughed, louder then.

"Ok, I was really upset. I asked her what was going on, what Mason had been thinking. She said... she said she didn't know- that she was just as upset as I was, but, I didn't believe her. Mason, who was like our own kid, had gotten this big hockey contract and I knew that she was so excited for him about that. I didn't understand how if she really loved you how she could even be a little bit excited when you were so heartbroken. So I told her that."

"Oh, mom."

"I know. It was very unfair of me, but I was so upset. I knew how much you loved him, how much we all loved him, and honey- I really thought you guys were going to get married, you thought that too. It hit me just as hard as it hit you."

Stephen cleared his throat again.

"Ok, ok. Not just as hard, but... hard."

"Was she mad at you?"

"No, I don't think, not really. She understood why I was upset. But then she said something like she wasn't going to stay on the line and be upset with her son for making a decision about his future, and then, well, I didn't handle that well at all. I told her that I thought we needed a break as well."

Stephen was chuckling now.

"Stephen!"

"Dad!"

"It was immature," Caroline conceded. "You know, I think it was a lot of things for me. I was really insecure. I know that now. John and Judy had this huge business, and they were doing so well. Your dad was moving up in the Police Department and had just become Staff Sergeant, and I had already started to feel like I was losing my place. I had taken so much pride in being your mom, and I was already really struggling with you moving away. I knew Scarlett was going to be right behind you, and then having you move away sad? It made me feel like I had failed as a mom, like I had disappointed you somehow."

"Mom." Sadie reached over and put her hand on her mom's arm.

"Oh, I know. It seems silly now, but I had a really hard time there for a while. Your dad was so good to me. He let me have my moment. When we got on that plane to come back home after dropping you off that first Fall, it was awful. I cried the whole flight home, and then for a few days after that. I missed you so much."

"What happened with Judy?"

"I missed her too. I knew she had dropped Mason off across the country and that wouldn't have been easy either, even though she was more used to it by then than I was. I was lamenting about it to Stephen one night. It had been just over a month, more than that I guess, it was close to Thanksgiving... and he told me that if I didn't walk over there and apologize right then that he was going to go over by himself, and the three of them would hang out without me."

"Dad."

Stephen shrugged from behind his paper. "Sometimes a little tough love does the trick."

"He was right, it worked. I said I was sorry, she said she was sorry, even though she had nothing to be sorry about and we hugged. I cried with her on her couch."

"There was a lot of crying that year," Stephen added.

Caroline chuckled, "There was. But it was good. I told her that I just wanted to see you happy, and she knew that, she felt like she lost you too. We will always love each other's children, no matter what, no matter who *they* love."

"That's really nice."

"Absolutely, and we promised that we would always be honest with each other about how we were feeling. I was sad for you when Mason brought a new girl home."

"Wait, what? He did!?"

"Yep, the following year. Judy said that they had been dating a couple of months but that she didn't think it was too serious. Pretty girl too. She adored him. I had gone over for my weekly visit and I didn't know he was going to be there, and he didn't know I was coming. He looked sheepish, but I hugged him and told him I was happy for him."

"You never told me that."

"For what reason would I ever tell you that?"

"Seriously!?" Sadie was stunned, retroactively jealous.

"Yes. You had just started feeling better, had been on a few dates yourself if I can recall, so I left it alone. I'm sure you would have found out if it had turned into something serious. I wanted to protect your heart... it doesn't matter anyway. Judy told me a few weeks later that they had broken up. Didn't give a reason, just that Mason said it hadn't felt right."

"I can't believe you never said anything."

Caroline shrugged.

"The next hard conversation Judy and I had was when I told her you were getting married. Then she was the one crying. She had always hoped you and Mason would find your way back together."

Sadie thought about that for a while before saying anything. "She came to the wedding."

"Of course she did. She loves you."

"I remember her there. It felt weird."

"For everyone." Caroline added.

"Caroline!"

"Mom!" Sadie exclaimed.

"What!? It was! I told you that then. It felt fast."

"It was." Sadie nodded.

"But that man has brought me two of the most beautiful grandchildren the world has ever seen, so I will forever be grateful to him, for that."

Sadie gave a nod. "Agreed."

It was then that the kids started arguing upstairs, and Stephen stood, saying he would handle it. The women sat and listened quietly as Stephen used his 'cop voice' going up the stairs. "Now listen here you two!" It was quiet for a moment and then they heard a fit of giggles. Sadie laughed.

"Changing the topic," Caroline continued, "what made you decide to come to church this morning?" She looked at her watch, making sure they weren't going to be late.

"Something Emily said last night." When Caroline didn't say anything, Sadie continued, "She said she misses me and wants to see me happy. She said I need to start praying again."

"I always liked that girl."

"I know... and for the first time in a long time, I wondered if maybe she was right. I've been mad, you know? I can't believe Nick just left, and a big part of me has blamed God, but what if it wasn't God? What if it was me? Or Nick? What if God still wants me to talk to him?"

"Oh Sade."

"I know. Maybe I've been so unsettled for so long *because* I stopped talking to him. Emily was right about the divorce group, it's been helpful. And when she told me I should pray, my immediate internal reaction was 'yes please', which you know, isn't that a sign?"

"I would think so. Sadie, God has never left you alone. He's right here. I don't understand why you think any of what happened was God's fault?"

"Because mom, I never wanted to marry him in the first place."

Chapter Twenty Three

Now

Sadie covered her mouth with her hand, shocked that she had just said that out loud.

Caroline's eyes could not physically get any bigger. She suddenly stood, "Stephen!" She yelled. "Sadie and I are taking her car to church. Pack up the kids and meet us there."

Once she heard his 'Sure thing!' she looked at Sadie. "Let's go. I'll drive."

They got in the car and Caroline started driving. She was quiet for a long time, giving Sadie space. Sadie was staring out of the window, watching the familiar houses and fields pass by. Her mind was tired from continually processing the last few weeks. A lot had happened since she attended that first church meeting with Emily. She had started thinking about things differently, she was ready to do the work to figure out why she was feeling like she was feeling, she had even run into Mason, heck, he had asked her out. When she told Emily, Emily was thrilled and told her she'd been stupid for not calling him already.

She couldn't believe she had come out and just said that to her mom. She had thought it so much since Nick left, she was actually more surprised she hadn't said anything before now. Again, probably self-preservation, wanting to avoid the embarrassment and keep her anger at bay.

Five minutes into the drive, her mom interrupted her thoughts "Sadie, honey. Do you want to talk about it? We've got time."

Caroline had always been the one person in Sadie's life that she could be completely honest with without fear of repercussion. In her teenage years Sadie acted as if her mom would always just be there, that her presence was a given. There was no doubt that she loved her mom, but she knew now that back then it had been very much a one-way relationship. She had talked to her mom when she wanted to and ignored her when she didn't. She went in for a hug when she needed one and pushed her mom away when she didn't. She would call her when she needed something and wouldn't call her unless she did. It wasn't until Sadie got to university that first year that she realized that her mom wasn't always just going to be there. She wasn't standing there, asking for a hug. Sometimes she would call home and Caroline wasn't even home; she had no way to talk to her unless Caroline made herself available. But even then, her mom had always made herself available. She had never appreciated her mom as much as when she realized her mom wasn't always going to be right there, and she felt full of gratitude now that her mom was sitting here beside her. Her hesitation in sharing with her mom didn't come from fear of her mom's response, it came from not wanting to let her mom down.

Sadie sighed and turned to her mom. "It's embarrassing, it's going to sound like I'm making excuses."

"For what?"

"For marrying Nick. For getting a divorce."

Caroline waited, when her daughter provided nothing else, Caroline continued, "Sade, when you called and said that you and Nick were getting married, your dad and I were shocked, Scarlett was shocked. You had only been dating him for six months and I asked you then what the rush was. We had only met him once and while he seemed like a nice enough guy, it *did* seem fast. I remember you getting really upset with me when I asked you what the rush was."

"I remember."

"So why honey, why did you marry him if you didn't really want to? Did he pressure you?"

Sadie laughed now, a sad laugh. She looked at her mom. "Can you pull over?"

Caroline did, the move from pavement to gravel jostling the car. She turned the ignition off and turned toward her daughter.

Sadie took a deep breath and looked up at her mom. "We argued a lot after I told you we were getting married."

"I remember."

"I was frustrated mom. I thought I was doing the right thing; I really believed it. Nick was a couple of years older than me and at the beginning we were really happy. He was fun and different from Mason. He seemed older, more mature. He loved talking about Seaside Studio and had some great ideas about expanding the business, you know he's part of the reason it's as big as it is today. For the first time in a long time I was beginning to see a life after Mason. I saw us as kind of this power couple. I would take the lead on the creative side of the Studio and he would manage the business. I wanted that for me, for us. He was willing to move back to Nova Scotia with me and we dreamed of travelling the world, taking pictures and entering art shows. But there was one issue with us, and I couldn't figure it out."

"Ok..."

"He wanted our relationship to be more... physical."

Caroline's eyebrows scrunched together.

"We had been dating for a while, and I thought he was so good looking. I had gone days, sometimes weeks without thinking about Mason. Mom, that was huge."

Caroline offered a sympathetic smile.

"But he wanted more than what I was willing to give him, in that way. He never pressured me, but it ended up coming up, a lot. I would stop things when I felt like they were going too fast and he was fine with it for the first while, but then he would be talking about our life together, and would bring up how sex is an important part of a relationship... I was a virgin, Mason and I had never crossed that line. But also, a part of me really didn't know if I had disappointed Mason in that way. Like maybe even though he hadn't said anything that he had wanted something more than what I could give. When we broke up, I thought that maybe he wanted to date other people and that's immediately where my head went. He wants more than what I can give. And I didn't want the same thing to happen with Nick, that I just keep losing people I care about because I wouldn't just grow up."

"Sadie."

"I know. I'm telling you my thoughts then. And, I had been to church long enough to know that sex is for marriage, for your husband." She looked at her mom again, who now had tears in her eyes. Sadie shrugged, "so I talked to him about getting married, a lot. He wasn't interested in that, *also* said it was too fast by the way, but then graduation was coming and there were times when we were talking about our plans when getting married did make sense. I wasn't going to live with him before getting married. And I knew he wasn't a Christian, but I was, so I knew what I should be doing. And I know the bible talks about marrying another Christian but he was coming to church with me each week. He knew what I believed and he supported it, supported me, not everyone I had gone on dates with before that were interested in that part of my life. So in my mind, if he came to church, he would eventually come to know God. And if we got married before we had sex, then I would not be sinning."

"Oh Sadie," She could see her mother's heart breaking in front of her, only a foot away.

"And so one night when we were having dinner, he proposed. And my first reaction was fear. Not happiness or excitement, or even love. But I knew I had been the one to ask for this, pushed for it even, so what was I supposed to do? I said yes. And I hung onto the parts that I was looking forward to. Being done school, adulting, growing the business, moving on, and doing it in the right way, in a way that pleased God."

Caroline took a deep breath.

"And then, well you know how it went. Things were great in the beginning. He liked it here in Darlings, business was good. But then it was like he woke up one day and wondered how he ever got here. And I wondered the same thing and we tried to work through it. He started talking about Ontario way more. I was thrilled when almost right away I found out I was pregnant, but I could tell Nick was more scared than happy. He left working for the Studio to go to the bank, which made no sense, he was making more money with me, but he said he needed some space, that we couldn't live together and work together and raise kids together, and then I started getting upset, it was *literally* why I married him, because of that dream we had. And then when he left, I was just so mad at God. Like WHY!? I did this for Him." She shook her head. "I couldn't tell anyone the real reason I was getting married, because I was afraid you would try to stop me, and if you stopped me then what was I even doing? I was going to be single, and a virgin, forever? I was done university, there was no one else."

"That you knew of then."

"Right."

"I'm so sorry Sadie. I wish I would've known all of that."

"I know, and trust me, there were thousands of times over the last 10 years when I wish I would have told you. That someone would have called it all off for me. So stupid."

"That's a lot."

Sadie chuckled. "It is a lot. And now that I can at least acknowledge how I got here, I can figure out how to get through it."

"I'm so proud of you."

"Thanks mom. I'm sorry for not sharing everything with you before now. I've probably not been the most fun person to be around these last few years."

"No, I wouldn't say that at all. I would say you've been very... introspective. Which is important too, you know. We all go through different things Sadie, and part of learning and growing into wise women is to take stock of where you've been, what you've been through, and what you've learned from it, and then decide how you'll use that knowledge going forward. People that don't do that spend their whole lives spiraling and feeling sorry for themselves and it's really no way to live, or to love others around you. You're doing the hard work and it may very well impact not just yourself and your children, but generations to come."

She smiled at her mom, "Sheesh, that's deep."

Caroline laughed, "Well, yes. I'm working on becoming the little wise old lady that sits on her porch in her rocking chair reading her bible."

"Your life goal."

"My life goal. And I want you there right beside me. We will eventually be old and grey at the same time you know."

Sadie laughed, "Before I turn grey, maybe I can at least get to church. I have some things to sort out with God."

Caroline smiled, pride bursting through her heart. "That sounds wonderful."

Chapter Twenty Four

Now

Tuesday of that week Sadie was in her office, reviewing online proofs of photographs her team had submitted to her for publishing, and preparing for her meeting with Levi at the arena, when she received a pop-up notification on her screen, indicating she had received a new email from Emily. Sadie had felt energized from the weekend, a fun Saturday night with Emily followed by a Sunday that had been emotionally exhausting, but had filled her cup. She had talked to her mom and had gone back to church, real church, and it had felt really good. She couldn't believe she had let Tess and Jacob go for so many years without her. Instead of beating herself up about it, she reminded herself that that was then and this was now, and she needed to focus on the now, reliving the past wasn't a throughway for joy. And then last night she had gone to another DivorceCare meeting where she participated fully and engaged in the conversation around ways to move forward. She knew now more than ever that she wanted to talk to Mason.

She stood to stretch and kicked off her heels in the process. With a business meeting this morning, Sadie had spent time on her makeup, ensuring it was professional and light, and had pulled her hair up into a bun. With her red pencil skirt and matching jacket, she looked like the girl boss that she was. She loved dressing up now and when she looked in the mirror, reminded herself to do it more.

She was excited about this meeting. Seaside studios had different forms of their artwork hanging from fisherman's museums and commercial fishing vessels in Nova Scotia to art galleries and museums in British Columbia, but it had always been important to Sadie that their work remain accessible to anyone. To have the opportunity to hang her photographs in the offices of their local arena felt significant and would be something she would be proud of.

A few hours later, Sadie left her meeting at the arena with Levi having agreed to sell him six enlarged photographs- four framed for offices and one for each of the two large boardrooms. They had also agreed on local artist Samanatha Jenkins to paint one of Sadie's photographs as a large mural in the lobby, and Samantha, who as it turns out was a big fan of Sadie's work, had agreed to the terms of the proposed contract. They made a tentative plan for Sam to start the work in the coming weeks and prepared a tentative press release for December 23rd, with Levi, Sadie and Sam having their picture taken in front of the completed mural. Sadie's Marketing Manager Stephanie would handle the press release.

Sadie felt like celebrating and she would have taken the kids out for supper, but Tess had gone to a friends after school and was getting a ride to ballet from there, and Jacob had been invited to another friend's house to make Halloween costumes.

Halloween was this coming Friday, and it was a day Sadie had never really enjoyed. Her parents had always taken her and Scarlett trick-or-treating when they were younger, but there was never much build up to it or talk about it afterwards. Now, she lived too far out of town to get any trick-or-treaters, just like her parents had when she was younger, and her kids had always wound up over-tired and over-stimulated. Each year she thought it would get better, but each year it hadn't. This year though, the kids had each been asked to go to different trunk-or-treats around town with friends from church, and then stay at their house for a sleepover. Knowing the families, Sadie had readily agreed and looked forward to a night alone, something that rarely happened without having to ask her parents for a favour. She had already planned to buy a bottle of wine, a new pair of pajamas, and she was going to settle in and catch up on some tv shows that had been recommended to her but that she never got around to watching.

Given that she had the afternoon to herself now as well, she decided to take a drive over to her parents and fill them in on how things had gone with Levi. She left the arena and took the scenic route, driving down Water Street, past the empty and quiet wharves where boats bobbed in wait. In the coming weeks the wharves around this end of the province would be coming back to life, filling with dozens of trucks and trailers loaded with traps, captains and crewmen ensuring they have all they need, hired tradespeople ensuring that each boat is mechanically sound and ready for the season ahead. The energy found amongst each other and the 24/7 pop-up stations of coffee and donuts, would carry men and women through another season of hard work. She was proud of where she was from and loved having ties to such a cool community, such a unique livelihood. Approaching the town limit, she drove past stretches of homes that sat close to the sidewalk, the homes seemingly backing up the farther you drove from the town's center. Within only a couple of minutes she was driving past large farmhouses and fields filled with cows lying next to round ton bales. She smiled as she passed a moving tractor, a little boy sitting on the lap of the farmer as they made their way through his field.

The sun was still high in the sky and as she drove further from town, past the fields and towards the lake where her parents lived, she found herself once again thinking about Mason, the boy she had once desperately loved. Once the shock of seeing him again had worn off, she had found herself wondering how he was doing, really doing, and she realized that there were things that she wanted to say to him. He had asked her to get together, and she knew now that if he asked her again she would say yes, but he hadn't given her his phone number, and she hadn't shared hers. She guessed that one of them would eventually find a way to reach out, but the anticipation of it had consumed her thoughts for the last few days. She thought she might see him in church yesterday, but the church had two Sunday morning services, and she heard that he had gone to the earlier one, while her family and her parents had gone to the later one. There was still a buzz among the congregation that he had been there, a celebrity citing of sorts. Darlings followed hockey closely, and Mason had made the town proud, even after his injury. His name was brought up by players and parents alike in rinks across the province, an example of what players could become if they worked hard.

Sadie pulled into her parent's yard and noticed that their vehicles weren't home. She hadn't called ahead and had assumed that one of them would be there, as they usually were. From the back seat she grabbed her bag with her sneakers and change of clothes and carried it into the house. Realizing that no one was home, she changed into her matching joggers and hoodie, a bright blue pair that accentuated the deep brown of her hair. She made herself a coffee, laced up her sneakers and walked to the front porch that overlooked the lake. It was a beautiful afternoon and she sat on the porch swing watching the trout jump in the lake. She sipped her caramel flavoured coffee and said a silent prayer asking God to help her figure out what was next.

She was staring at the water and enjoying the quiet when she heard the wooden stairs that led to the side of the porch creek. She turned and couldn't believe that Mason was walking toward her, up her parents' stairs. He stopped at the end of the porch and leaned against the wooden column that joined the stairs to the deck, keeping his distance.

You look so good, Sadie thought now.

"Hi." Mason started. He didn't have a ball hat on and looked like he had just gotten out of the shower. His hair was wet, long enough to brush, short enough that she doubted it would flip under his hat. He was wearing jeans and a faded light blue crew neck sweater that looked well worn, rips along the collar and cuffs, still his style, she noted. He still had the scruff she noticed the first time she saw him, and her heart responded to seeing him by picking up speed. She didn't feel nervous as much as relieved that the wait to see him was over.

"Hi," She said now. Then, "How are you?"

He grinned. "Good. I hope you don't mind that I came over. I was down the road finishing my run when I saw your car pull in. I thought I'd take the chance to see if you were still here."

"Here I am"

"I see that," he smiled now, "I'm glad."

"You can run?"

"Yeah, slowly. I pace myself because I don't want to do anything to hurt my knee again, but yeah, I'm staying in the best shape that I can."

"I can see that."

He raised an eyebrow and chuckled. "Thanks."

After a long pause Sadie looked over at him, "Want to join me?" she gestured to the seat next to her and he nodded, making his way over.

He sat down next to her on the seat of the swing, and she felt the weight of his presence, physically as the swing shifted, but also emotionally, her heart responding to him as it always had, despite the hurt.

"Sadie," he started, just as she said, "Mason,"

They both stopped and smiled and he began again, staring at her, "Please, go ahead."

"First of all, I'm sorry for my outburst at the rink last week. I was really surprised to see you." When he didn't say anything, she continued. "Seeing you again, it's hard. But it's also good, you know? I don't know. In some ways it feels like my heart is betraying me by wanting to talk to you."

"Well... that sucks."

She chuckled again, "Yeah. It does. I'm not mad anymore Mason, not really. We were kids, you had every right to break up with me."

"Sadie."

"No, it's ok." She smiled at him and turned in her seat so she could really see him. She had some things she wanted to say to him and didn't know when she'd have the chance again.

He turned to look at her as well, his left arm coming up and resting on the back of the porch swing. They were close enough that he could touch her shoulder if he wanted to. He had never seen her hair up in a bun like that before and he couldn't believe how much older she looked, how naturally beautiful that she still was.

"I've done a lot of growing up myself you know." She continued, "I've made mistakes, my life took a direction I didn't think it would. But when I think about you? When I think about what we had... I'm grateful for it now, for that time together. Even if we weren't meant to be."

"Sadie,"

"I guess I just wanted to say that." She interrupted, before he could distract her from what she had to say. "You obviously know a lot of what happened in my life, heck, you coach my son's hockey team now...But I wasn't sure if you knew that I wasn't mad at you anymore, about high school, about Ontario, about the break up. And you definitely wouldn't have known after how I reacted last week. And lately, well, I've been really working through everything that's happened in my life, and the part I have to play in it, good and bad. I'm even working on my relationship with God," she grinned sheepishly. "It's been a ride, me and him, but when I think about being able to really move on, move onto the next chapter, I think about how important it is for me to try to close the chapter I'm in first, before I start another one. Kind of like when I journal... and when I think about Nick, I know that he is really happy in Ontario, and no amount of frustration is going to change that, so why spend my energy being frustrated?"

She paused, looking down in her lap and then back up at him. "I feel like I've lived my life in seasons. You and I, going to school and getting my degree, building my business, Nick, the kids... I've taken something from all of it and I want to learn how to close chapters and start new ones in a way that brings me back to who I used to be, but mixed in with who I am now. I want to be more fun and light, more go with the flow and less the girl who has to have everything planned and figured out at all times. I know that in order to do that I need to start closing some doors so that I can turn my attention to what's in front of me, to the ones I haven't opened yet."

"Ok..."

"Like, I've accepted that Nick's gone and I think I've finally forgiven him for leaving me; I'll never understand him leaving the kids, but the Nick and I chapter? I know that's closed. I'm glad he's where he wants to be and is happy. I'm happy here with Tess and Jacob. My business is still growing." She leaned in conspiratorially, "I'm actually sending a team of photographers to Spain this week to capture the small-scale fishing operations there, I've got the releases all drawn up and a connection I have there is going to host my guys. We're planning a big art exhibition here next year on what fishing looks like around the world. I want it to be inspirational, have our local fisherman take part in it. We have people coming from all across Canada to see it unveiled and I'm already so excited about it."

"Sadie, that's amazing."

"Thank you, but I got sidetracked... I guess I just wanted to say that because it's an example for me of a door opening, and I want to be present to focus on that. And when I think about other things that weigh on me, I always come back to you Mason. You were the other really important relationships in my life and I don't feel like I ever really got closure. I don't understand what happened with us, and I might never, and that's ok, but I *do* want you to know that I'm not mad anymore. It seems that it's an important step for me, for you to know that. I want to close that door but I think I can only do that when I know that you're ok, and that you and I are good."

She couldn't believe she was rambling like this, how easy it was to open up to a person that she hadn't spoken to in over 10 years. It was like they were right back to being the friends they were before they started dating all those years ago. His face was familiar and kind, and she knew now looking at him, that he cared about her. She could see it and she found comfort in that.

"Ok... well... I'm glad you're not mad, and yes, I'm good, but there are things that I think we still need to talk about Sadie." Mason could feel himself becoming increasingly anxious, an emotion he rarely experienced. He had to move, had to stand. He got up from the chair and walked to stand across from her. He leaned against the railing and folded his arms across his chest, hoping it would help calm him. He didn't want a door closed. That's the last thing he wanted.

He wanted the door open, wide open. He wanted to see Sadie on the other side of all of his doors.

She watched him thinking, feeling a little sad that he wanted to move farther away from her, but also knowing this would be their new reality. "I'm sorry. I overshare," she mumbled. Then taking a deep breath and looking up at him, "On that note, I start going to counselling this week, tomorrow actually, when Jacob is at hockey practice with you. It's been on the to-do list for a while and I decided I just needed to, well, do it. I found someone I didn't know. I have some things left to work out, about how to move on, and I need her help."

Mason was staring at Sadie and was dumbfounded on how to respond. Of course he wanted her to go to counselling if she needed it, but he didn't want her moving on, further away from him.

"That's good. I'm glad you're going. But Sadie," His intensity was probably freaking her out, "I think we need to talk about what happened, back after graduation. I didn't explain myself well then, I didn't know how. And I want to."

"Does it matter now though Mason? Really? It's been so long, we've both lived separate lives and look at us, we've been able to come back together, right back to where we grew up, and maybe we can even make our way back to being friends again. We both know we'll see each other around." She chuckled but noted that he wasn't smiling, so she stopped.

"Yes Sadie, it matters to me."

Chapter Twenty Five

Now

Stephen turned on the blinker of the RCMP cruiser, leaving the gravel road to turn onto his driveway. He drove through the forest of trees that provided both privacy and cover from the elements and coasted slowly towards his home. He had driven the whole way home on autopilot, he realized now, his mind occupied with his shift and all that had taken place. He had had another long day today and had to debrief with his team at the end of it, ensuring everyone was ok.

Two officers had been called to a home and ended up having to remove a little girl from it. The drug paraphernalia in the house had cost more than a year's worth of groceries and it was in no way safe for a child or an adult. As the youngest officer picked up the little girl to remove her from the situation, Stephen learned that she had begun sobbing, screaming for her mom, arms outstretched. Mom had been too strung out to notice that the little girl was crying, the drugs she had pushed through her arm erasing her comprehension of how loved she was, the awareness that she was needed- that she was this little girl's mother. The police had delivered the little girl to a dependable foster care family within the community, a family who had a long-standing reputation for taking in the most troubled kids and loving them well.

When the policemen had arrived back at the station, the senior officer came into the detachment to begin the paperwork. When the junior officer hadn't joined him, Stephen had found the young man sitting in the passenger seat of the cruiser with his head in his hands, weeping for the little girl and what he had just witnessed. Stephen, the staff sergeant and most respected man at the detachment had opened the driver's side door, got in, and sat quietly next to the young man while he cried. There wasn't anything Stephen could say to make it better for him, but he could be there in silent comradery. His heart took some relief in knowing that he was nearing retirement, but he wouldn't leave until he knew there would also be someone there to sit with his constables when they needed it.

He knew the general reputation that the RCMP had. That they were an arrogant bunch, on the lookout for places to wield their authority, but the general public had zero idea of the things these men and women experienced on a day-to-day basis. Nor how it broke them, and how that confidence they employed was a necessity if they wanted to get through the next hour, the next shift. There were days, like today, that sometimes they had reached their limit and their emotions took over. It was healthy, Stephen knew, and he wished more of his team would let themselves feel the things they experienced, also understanding that too much feeling, and feeling at the wrong time, would put them in harm's way. It was a tight walk and the ones who did it, he knew they did it for the desire to keep their communities safe, it wasn't worth it otherwise.

His heart took a small leap seeing Sadie's SUV in the driveway. Sadie had been back in Darlings for 10 years now and the four years before that, when she had been away to university were very hard on Caroline, but also very hard on him too. Sadie was his first-born daughter and the pride that he felt when he watched her move about the world he would never be able to explain.

He had only ever been truly angry once in his personal life and it was when Sadie had arrived at their home five years ago to tell them that she and Nick were separating. For the rest of his days, he'll never forget how she broke down in front of them as she shared some of the things she had been experiencing. Stephen was ashamed to think now that he had handled it by leaving the room. He just could not believe that anyone would treat his beloved daughter that way and if Nick hadn't already left town he would have been sure he had found his way out.

He parked his car next to Sadie's and entering the kitchen, took off his duty belt, leaving it on the kitchen table next to Sadie's duffle bag. When she didn't answer when he called, he made his way out to the porch to find her, and Mason, together outside.

"Sir." Mason stood straighter.

"Stand down son, you're fine. It's good to see you again." Then looking at Sadie, "Hi love."

"Hi Dad. Mason and I were just... catching up."

"Sounds good." He looked at Mason and then back to his daughter, "I'll be inside, let me know if you need anything."

"I'll be in in a minute."

Stephen turned to head back into the house and shut the patio door behind him.

"He doesn't like me." Mason began.

"He loves you. Both of my parents do."

"It doesn't feel that way."

"He's never said a bad thing about you," Sadie continued, "Even when I wanted him to." She smiled.

Mason moved back to sitting on the swing next to Sadie, turning to face her. He wanted more time with her, but knew he should probably go.

"So, can I see you again?"

Sadie was confused. "Why? I'm sure you have a lot going on. Starting a new job, hockey."

Mason cut her off, "Sadie, I want to see you again, if you'll let me. I want to talk to you, when I don't feel rushed and can have a real conversation with you. What are you doing this weekend?"

"It's Halloween."

"I hate Halloween," he said then. "I assume you're taking the kids out?"

"Me too. And no, actually. They are both going with friends this year. I actually have the night to myself." Sadie reached up and pulled the elastic out of her hair. Her hair, now crimped and messy, fell around her shoulders. "I was going to buy a box of Halloween candy and find a Christmas movie to watch and not get off the couch for four hours."

He looked at her, his heart picking up speed again. "That sounds... great actually."

She watched him next to her. So tall now, so much older, still so strong- she could see his shoulder muscles through his sweater. She started talking before she could talk herself out of it.

"Well...Mason, would you like to watch a Christmas movie with me? On Halloween?"

Hope rushed in and his stomach flipped. He pretended to think really hard about it. "Only if it's about a girl who comes home for Christmas with her big city boyfriend- the one who doesn't like to get dirty, and she- in a surprise to no one, falls in love with the guy who's too old to be single and owns the Christmas Tree farm."

She laughed unexpectedly, "You watch Hallmark movies!"

He laughed, "No, but I know the gist." Then they both realized what he had said, and how close to their real lives that fictional plot was. He kept going before it became awkward. "So, your house?"

"Yeah, if that's ok." He said that would be great. She figured he might know where she lived, but she gave him the address anyway. He pulled his phone out and she gave him her phone number and he gave her his in return. She told him he could come any time after six. Then she'd have a chance to get home from work, grab something to eat and get comfortable.

"That sounds great. What can I bring?"

"I have a bottle of wine and will pick up a box of Halloween candy."

She looked like the Sadie he had remembered and he was already nervous for Friday. He didn't know how he was going to make it through the next few days. The anticipation would kill him. "I'll bring a pizza... should... I wear my pajamas too?"

She laughed again. "Please no."

"If you say so." Then he smiled at her, a real genuine smile, then added, "Ok, lady Sadie, I'll see you later then."

He turned and jogged down the steps, hands in his pockets. He was halfway to the backyard path before she realized that he had used the nickname she hadn't heard in more than a decade, her face warming at the intimacy of the bygone moment.

Sadie sat there for a while on the swing and instead of feeling excitement about Friday, panic set in. What was she thinking? This wasn't shutting a door! Who did she think she was? What would people think? That Mason shows back up in town and she just jumps from one guy to the next? And what about her kids? She never gets a night alone and instead of using it for herself, something she definitely needed, she invites a man over? To watch a movie?! She rested her head on her knees. She had her first appointment with her counsellor tomorrow and felt a little better knowing she had someone objective to talk this all out with.

It was a few minutes of sitting with her own thoughts before she remembered her dad was inside. She had noticed tonight that he was looking even a little older, a little more tired. She stood and stretched, picking up her coffee cup, she slid open the back door. She wasn't ready to tell her dad, or anybody, about her plans with Mason on Friday, but she couldn't wait to fill him in on her new project at the arena.

For all the ways she knew she let her dad down, she wanted to keep finding ways to make him proud.

Chapter Twenty Six

Now

Sadie found her dad in his recliner, leaned back and eyes closed. He had changed out of his uniform and was wearing track pants and an old T-shirt with paint stains on it. She didn't remember the last time he had painted something...was that shirt part of his regular wardrobe? She smiled to herself and leaned down to give him a quick kiss on the head before she snuck out. The shock of seeing one eye slowly open as she leaned in towards him made her jump back and scream.

"Jeese dad! I thought you were sleeping!"

He sat up in his chair, kicking in the footrest until it clicked closed, turning it into a rocking chair again. "No, I was just resting my eyes."

She took the seat across from him, her back to the window that displayed the water. "How was your day?"

"It was a long one actually. I was just thanking God that I am able to come home to this house and to your mother. To find you here," he added, "is always a pleasant surprise."

She smiled.

"So Mason, eh?"

"Yeah. It was nice of him to come over. He just wanted to say hi."

He scrunched his eyebrows. "Ok."

"Ok, what?"

"It seemed to me that you guys were having an important conversation."

"He wants to talk, yeah."

"And..."

"And I will. I just want to be sure he knows that I just want to be friends, if anything."

"Why?"

"Why, what?" Sadie was confused, again.

"Why do you want to just be friends with him? I remember a time when you loved him very much. And I know he loved you."

Sadie was watching her dad. He was watching her back. They didn't have these kinds of conversations very often-ever, actually. They were close, but he had never talked to her about her relationships, they kept their conversations to the kids, their work and what was going on in their day to day.

"You think I should date him again?"

"I didn't say that. I asked you why *you* just want to be friends with him."

Sadie was never one who had to fill the silence, she got that from her dad she knew. She sat there and thought about it. She knew she still cared for Mason but so much had happened since those years so long ago. She turned and pulled her feet up on the couch so that she was still facing her dad but could also see out of the window. She stared now between the rope that held the porch swing and out towards the water. She wanted to move forward, not back, but she also wanted to do it under the radar, her family had been through enough drama because of her.

She looked back at her dad, her eyes suddenly wet and the emotion heavy in her voice. "I'm sorry, Dad."

"Sorry for what?" He had no idea where this was going.

"For everything. For marrying Nick, for getting a divorce. I know that's not what God wanted for me, or what you and mom wanted for me." She quickly swiped at the tears that had begun to fall. "I've never said anything because it's been so embarrassing, but so much has been coming up for me lately and I'm trying to work through it, but I never said I was sorry. I am. I know I embarrassed you and mom. You were left to tell people that my marriage failed, that I was raising kids on my own, that he left. I know people in the church talked about it. How hard that must have been for you."

Her chin was quivering, and she was doing her best not to completely break down, but she was also glad she was getting it off her chest, another step in the work she had to do, in healing.

Stephen slowly stopped his rocking and sat up in his chair, his elbows propping him up, so he was sitting up straight. "Sadie Marie Campbell, that is enough."

She was startled, she had upset him. She hated upsetting him.

"You do not owe me one apology and you never have. I can't believe you think that."

"Dad..."

"No!" His tone was forceful. This was his angry voice, the one that she had worked to avoid her whole life. She put her head in her hands, wishing she could disappear.

Stephen stood up. He was pacing now. He stopped in front of her.

"Sadie, look at me."

She looked up, the skin around her eyes were red and puffy and Stephen was startled to see how timid she looked. He took a step back, though still in front of her.

"Sadie." He began again, then lowered his voice a notch. "I am not upset with you. I am very upset that you would think that you have ever embarrassed me, or brought shame to this family. And shame on me for not saying this to you sooner, but Sadie, I am PROUD of you. I am so very proud of you."

Sadie looked at her dad and her heart began to slowly break. She could feel it coming apart in her chest.

"I have never been ashamed of you. Do you know how hard it is to get out of a difficult, unhealthy relationship? How brave that is? Sadie, honey. You could have stayed with Nick. You could have stayed and in many ways staying is easier than leaving. I see it all the time, every day. Women who hate conflict, who stay because they have a fear of being alone, for their kids- because they feel like it's the right thing to do, because they don't know what's next, but Sadie, deciding that you deserve better? That your children deserve better? That is not easy. It is not selfish, and it certainly DOES NOT bring me shame. I am proud of you Sadie. I am so proud of how you picked up the pieces after he left. I am proud of how you've loved your children. But what you did? What you're doing now? That is hard."

"Dad…" Sadie's eyes were blurry from the tears that wouldn't stop coming. When she looked at her dad, she saw three of him.

"No, let me finish. I know only some of what you've dealt with. To hear people talk about you, to be made to feel that they're talking about you when you're not around? Those people were never in your home. To have people tell you that they feel bad for your kids? THAT is hard Sadie. But it doesn't make what you did wrong. Many people don't leave when they should. You did. Your children will have a completely different upbringing than they would have if you had stayed in a marriage where you were constantly being put down, made to feel small, controlled… abused. Nobody knows anyone's whole story and whenever… WHENEVER someone has mentioned you to me, Sadie, my voice, my heart, it *fills* with pride. I am so proud that you're my daughter. And I am so so sorry that I didn't say this to you before." His voice cracked. He was not an emotional man, but the thought that his daughter thought that he was ashamed of her? He didn't know if he could take it.

"But… what about God? The bible says divorce is a sin."

"Of course it is! Have you suffered through this? Going through a divorce? Building a life with someone using super glue, only to have it slowly ripped apart, piece by piece. Has that been enjoyable for you?" He stopped and kneeled in front of her. "Sadie, would you want Tess going through what you went through?"

She looked at her dad's face. She had wiped away the tears. The boulder that had been in her throat moved to her stomach, the thought of Tess in a relationship like hers made her feel sick.

"No."

"And would you want her to stay in a relationship that was like yours and Nick's?"

The tears came again, "Absolutely not."

"No, of course not! And God didn't want that for you either. You are His daughter Sadie. I share you with Him. Divorce is a sin because He knows that it hurts you from the inside out. That's what sin does. No matter the sin, and we all sin Sadie, every one of us. And God tells us sin is wrong because it hurts Him and it hurts us. Every Christian has to deal with that. All of us. You're not special in that regard."

She chuckled then. It came unexpectedly and the boulder that had been in her chest started to crack.

"Sadie, I know how hard you worked on your marriage. I know how hard you tried. I am so proud of you for that. But please, please for the love of God, for God's love, please don't let what you went through stop you from being happy. The devil rejoices when that happens. Satan wins every time someone's identity becomes the sin instead of being the son or daughter of The One who died for that sin."

"Dad..." Sadie stood and wrapped her arms around her dad. She had never loved him more. "I love you."

"I love you too kiddo. Always"

They heard the screen door slam and looked up to see Caroline standing there holding a paper bag, celery stalks sticking out of the top.

"Hey now... what's going on?" She could see Sadie had been crying, and Stephen looked like his blood pressure was sky high.

Sadie looked at her dad, neither knew what to say.

"I signed a new deal with Levi at the arena," Sadie sniffed, "He bought a bunch of my photographs and Samantha Jenkins is going to paint a mural of one of my photographs in the lobby."

Stephen looked at his daughter and raised his eyebrows, placing his hand on the back of her shoulder.

"I was just telling her how proud of her I was, how proud of her I am." Stephen added.

"Well, yes of course," Caroline responded, concern evident in her voice as she began pulling groceries from the bag, "but if you're getting this emotional over the thought of a mural, I can't imagine how you'll react once it's actually painted."

Sadie and Stephen looked at each other and both started laughing. They made their way toward the kitchen to help with supper. As the three of them talked about their day, Sadie watched her parents move around the kitchen together, like a choreographed dance only the two of them knew. As she listened and watched, she couldn't help but feel the walls she had built around her heart so long ago start to come down.

Chapter Twenty Seven

Now

Jacob and Tess were extra chatty this afternoon when Sadie picked them up from school. They were in the same class and their music teacher had tasked them with interviewing an adult about music they loved from their childhood. Sadie had been telling them about some of the music she had loved when she was a teenager and when they asked if they could hear it, she hadn't even been sure it would be on Spotify. She picked up her phone, scanned for 'Jesus Freak' by DC Talk and sure enough, there it was. She turned it on and as the kids listened, neither could believe their mom knew all the words to a song they had never even heard of before. She laughed and turned it up loud, the kids catching on to the chorus quickly. When the song ended, she turned on 'Only Wanna Be With You' by Hootie and the Blowfish and it was blaring through the vehicle when she turned into the rink and pulled up next to the entrance. She popped the trunk while Jacob hopped out to grab his gear.

The music had been turned up so loud that she didn't hear Jacob yell 'hey coach!' as the trunk door slowly closed. She was singing along and looking for other songs she could share with Tess when an arm came up and rested itself on her door where her window was rolled down.

"Hey."

"Ah!" She screamed. "You scared me!"

Mason chuckled. "Lovely voice."

She rolled her eyes, temporarily forgetting Tess was sitting right behind her.

Mason pulled back laughing and double tapped his fist on the window ledge of the door panel before walking towards the rink, looking back at her smiling, he called out, "I'm looking forward to Friday!"

She smiled at him and shook her head. She saw him wait for Jacob to hold the door for him, and she went back to her phone.

"What's going on Friday?" a small voice came from behind her.

Sadie stopped scrolling. She didn't immediately respond but knew how she responded mattered. She put down her phone and turned around in her seat so she could see Tess who was now staring at her.

"Jacob's coach and I are going to hang out on Friday."

"Why?" Tess's response was cold.

"Because we used to be friends. And we'd like to be friends again."

Tess looked at her mom. "Is he your boyfriend?"

"What? No Tess. Why would you ask that?"

"Because Connor said that his mom said that you and their coach used to be boyfriend and girlfriend and then that you probably would be again."

"Tess, Mason- Jacob's coach... him and I, we are just friends." She was going to kill Connor's nosy good-for-nothing mother.

"But are you going to date him?"

She never wanted to lie to her daughter, she also didn't want her to worry for naught. She took off her seatbelt and turned completely around. "Tess, honey. Mason and I dated a really long time ago. A lot has happened since then."

"Like me."

"Like you." Sadie conceded.

"And like dad."

Sadie paused. "Yes, and like dad. And that means that we have a lot of things to talk about, to catch up on."

Tess was looking out of the window, no longer at Sadie.

"I miss dad."

"I know you do, baby."

"If you start dating Jacob's coach, you and Dad will never get back together." Her chin was quivering.

Sadie turned back around and put the vehicle in drive. She pulled it away from the arena entrance and whipped it into the nearest parking spot. She turned the car off, opened her door and went around to the back seat where Jacob had been sitting just a few moments ago. She crawled in next to her daughter, both of them in the backseat, Tess's eyes wide.

"Mom, what are you doing?"

"I want to talk to you, and not when I can't see you. Come here."

Tess scooted over and sat next to her mom. It was times like these where Sadie despised Nick, she would never understand him leaving this little girl.

Sadie turned Tess so that she could see her. "Tess, honey. You know that there is no one in the whole world that I love more than you? More than Jacob?"

"Yeah." Tess said it like she knew what the right answer was, but that she didn't believe it to be true.

"Tess, look at me honey. There is no one who I love more than you and your brother. And do you know who I have to thank for you two?"

"God?"

Sadie smiled. "Yes, God. And do you know who else?"

"Dad?"

"Yes! Your dad. He gave me you and for that reason he will always be so special to me. I am so happy you're my daughter. And he helped give me that."

"Ok."

"But Tess," Sadie continued, her daughter looking up at her. *God, please help me.*

"I need you to know that your dad and I are not going to date again. We are not going to get back together."

Tess's eyes welled with tears and she looked down, "I know."

Sadie felt for her. "You do?"

"Yeah. Jacob told me. I don't think he wants dad back though. I do."

"We would all like to see your dad more Tess. Having him away is hard."

Tess nodded.

"You know, you are going through something that I never had to go through. My parents, Grammy and Grampy, they are still together so all of these emotions you're feeling, I have never had to experience them." She looked down at Tess who was hanging off her every word, "I want to help you the best way I know how to, but sometimes mommy doesn't do a very good job of knowing what I can do to help. To make it hurt less."

"I know."

"What I can tell you, is that I am always going to be here. I am always going to love you and I am always going to be thankful for your dad Tess, even if I do start dating someone else."

"Do you think you will? Date someone else?"

"Yeah, I think so, someday. I'm pretty cool right?"

Tess smiled, and nodded.

"But Tess I promise you that if I ever do, I will talk to you about it first, ok? Mason and I are going to hang out on Friday as friends. He used to be my very best friend. Did you know that? When I was your age actually."

"No, I didn't."

"And when we got older we did start dating. It would be like if you and Reed started dating." Reed had been in school with Tess and Jacob since pre-school and had been over to the house often to play with them both.

"Eww!"

Sadie laughed. "Yes, well, it might not be so 'eww' when you're older. Come here, I want to hug you."

Tess crawled right up on her mom's lap, temporarily forgetting she was almost 11 now.

"I love you Tess," she whispered in Tess's ear. "And when I do start dating again, it will only be to someone who I know will love you and Jacob just as much as I do. Okay? I promise."

"Okay."

"And I want you to come talk to me whenever you have something to say ok? Even if you think it will hurt my feelings. I like knowing what you're thinking so that I can be a better mom to you."

"Okay... And mom?"

"Yeah?"

"Jacob's coach seems nice. And happy."

"He does, doesn't he?"

"Yeah, And I want you to be happy too. Just don't... forget about me."

Sadie looked down at Tess and couldn't contain the love she had for this brown haired, brown eyed, fair skinned little girl. She slowly began squeezing Tess, so hard that Tess started to scream, "Mom!"

"I will never forget about you." She kept squeezing, "I will love you and hug you and kiss you and squeeze you forever and ever."

Tess laughed and finally escaped her mom. "Don't you have a meeting to go to?"

"Oh crap!" Sadie hopped out of the car and ran around to the driver's seat. She forgot she was dropping off Tess at Aunt Scarlett and Uncle Pete's so that she could go to counselling. As she started the car and pulled out of the arena, she was thankful for that moment with Tess. It was a good reminder that Tess and Jacob, even when they were quiet, were also processing some of the same things she was. *Another thing to talk to Dr. Marsden about,* she thought now.

Chapter Twenty Eight

Now

Sadie's cell phone started ringing the second she pulled out of Scarlett's driveway. Recognizing the tone, she answered it through her steering wheel, and Emily's voice suddenly filled the car.

"Hey Sade, what are you up to?"

"Just dropped off Jacob and Tess and am headed to my counsellor for the first time. Trying not to freak out."

"Oh, that's awesome! You'll do great."

"Yeah, I hope so. What if I don't like her, or get good vibes from her?"

"Then you'll get someone else."

"Ugh."

"You'll be fine."

"What's going on with you?"

"I just wanted to know the plan for Friday, are we taking the kids around again?"

"Umm... no, not this year. They're going with friends."

"No! What!? Who am I going to steal candy from then??" Emily sounded hurt.

"Go buy your own candy!" Sadie laughed, "That's what I'm doing. I have a 50 pack of snickers staring me in the eye right now."

"Yum! Ok, I'll come over Friday and help you eat them. Up for a little Hocus Pocus?"

"Well... actually. I can't."

"Why not?"

Sadie was silent before she answered. Knowing Emily and knowing how she was about to react, she turned down the volume of her car speaker. "Mason's coming over."

After a beat of silence... "WHAAAT!!!??"

Sadie smiled, "It's not a big deal. We were talking at mom and dads."

"He was at your mom and dad's?"

"He popped over."

"He just popped over?"

"Yes. And we got to talking, and decided that since the kids were gone Friday, we would hang out."

"Hang out!?"

"Yes."

"At your house? Alone!?"

"Yes Em," Sadie chuckled. "I'm sure it will be fine."

"Oh... I'm sure it WILL be fine."

"Ok, bye Emily. Love you."

"I can't believe you didn't tell me."

"Bye Em! Pulling into counselling now! Gotta go!" She ended the call before she could hear the friendly protesting from the other line.

She backed into a parking spot, facing a building that on a quick drive-by could have easily been mistaken for someone's home. The beautiful Queen Anne Revival house blended in with others on the street, though large glass doors with fancy white script indicating the Doctor's name and hours she worked confirmed she was in the right place.

It was an odd feeling going somewhere in your hometown that you've never been to before, to meet someone you've never met before. Her feelings leading into the meeting had ranged from excited, to nervous, to almost cancelling, to calling to ask if there was an earlier time available (there wasn't), and now that she was here and was due to go in, she felt frozen.

Sadie's health plan included counselling sessions and once she finally acknowledged to herself that counselling could help her, she had logged in through the online portal to find a therapist in her area. Surprisingly, Darlings Lake and the surrounding area had more options than she thought they would. Because there were so many types of therapists, Sadie had to scroll through the available options, indicating via a checkbox what was important to her in a counsellor.

She had only two priorities in choosing a counsellor, she wanted it to be a woman, and she didn't want someone who had 'Christian counselling' as their specialization as had been suggested by Emily, Hattie, and her mom. She felt guilty enough about her divorce. She just wanted to be able to help her children with the loss of their dad, and she wanted some tangible scientifically proven strategies that she could implement each day in order to help with all of that, to help her move forward. She didn't want to be told that she should pray more, or what different bible verses said about it. She knew those things and could do that on her own. She wanted to know what her exact next steps should be.

Dr. Melanie Marsden was on the list, a psychologist who specialized in grief, family, and relationship counselling. Perfect, Sadie had thought. There was a picture of Dr. Marsden posted on the website and she had looked to Sadie to be slightly older than her mom was, another plus. She had wanted someone with experience and not someone who she thought went home and scrolled on her phone all night.

Walking into the lobby, she felt good as she opened the glass door, a light aroma of cinnamon wafting in the air. She looked around, noting a reception area that had been painted a very dark burgundy color, making the room feel smaller than it was. Couches and chairs covered in blankets and pillows were placed around the room and she could see down the hall at least three white doors with different names on them. The receptionist at the front desk asked her name and told her to have a seat. She was only a couple of minutes early, enough time to pull out the notes she had made about the things she wanted to talk about. She was reading through them for the third time when Dr. Marsden called for her from the entrance. Sadie smiled and stood, suddenly nervous again. Dr. Marsden walked Sadie to her office, making small talk along the way.

Dr. Marsden's office was very minimal. Painted lighter than the lobby, there was a couch off to the side, but the room also held two oversized rocking chairs. The doctor sat in one, indicating that Sadie should take the other. Sadie suddenly felt like she was right where she was supposed to be, and she realized that she looked forward to talking to someone new about what she had been dealing with, more than she had even realized.

"Sadie. It's so nice to meet you." Dr. Marsden began.

"It's nice to meet you too. Thank you for seeing me."

"Of course." The doctor did not seem in a rush. She was dressed professionally, but she appeared just as relaxed as she did professional, her calmness relaxing Sadie. Sadie was reminded that Hattie had made her feel the same way. Sadie wasn't sure how to start; she had never been to a counsellor before.

"Why don't you tell me why you wanted to come in. I think that's a good place to start." Dr Marsden said, as if reading her mind.

"Well, it's all a bit of a long story. I'm not sure how much detail you want to hear."

"Ok. Let me ask you this. If you had only one goal for our time together, what would it be?"

Sadie thought about it, but she knew where she'd like to start. "I'd like to be able to look forward to the future."

"OK then." The doctor smiled.

Sadie looked sheepish. "I know that's a big ask. I have a really good life, but I can't seem to be present in it, to enjoy what I have. I own my own business, it's doing really well. And I have two kids, Jacob and Tess. They are 10, almost 11, and they are both healthy, and fairly happy, I think. I live near my sister and parents and everyone is healthy. I went through a divorce about five years ago now and I can't seem to move forward. I'm always thinking about what went wrong or how things could have been different."

"Oh, I'm sorry. You didn't want to get divorced?"

"No, I think I did. I know I did. That's part of my problem."

"Why is that a problem? If it's something you wanted, I mean?"

Sadie noticed and appreciated that the question was a genuine one, and for such a simple question, it took her off guard. She sat in the rocking chair for almost a solid minute thinking about the answer.

"I don't know." Sadie finally answered and could feel her face start to heat, what it always did before she started crying. She had told herself that she would not cry today. She was going to come in here, share what was on her mind, get some good tips on how to change her outlook and check counselling off the to-do list. Becoming emotional wasn't on today's plan.

"Alright. Let's go back to all of those good things you have in your life, your work and your kids, your family. Why do you think it is that you're not looking forward to the future?"

"I guess I just feel really guilty. All the time. I grew up in *the church*," Sadie said then, emphasizing the last part, as if that would explain everything, "and I wasn't supposed to get divorced. The bible says not to, and I keep coming back to that. Every time I start to feel some level of happiness, it's like I'm reminded 'yeah Sadie, but you also got divorced.'"

The doctor squeezed her eyebrows together, frowning.

"And there's no way that everyone that's ever gotten divorced is walking around miserable, so I don't know why I am."

"How is your relationship with God?"

Sadie frowned. That was an odd question for her to ask.

"With God?" Sadie clarified. Maybe she misheard.

"Yes, you said you grew up in the church, and it sounds like you know what the bible says about divorce. The next logical question, for me, is how you view God."

This opened up a flood gate and not unlike air slowly being let out of a balloon, Sadie began sharing. If Dr. Marsden wanted to know what Sadie thought about God, she would tell her. The doctor took notes as Sadie talked about her strong faith as a teenager and then getting her heart broken in High School, the importance she placed on staying a virgin until she was married, and then about meeting Nick. She explained why she felt that she had to marry him and how God had really disappointed her when things didn't work out. She talked about Nick moving away, and about her being alone with the kids and how scared she was that they were going to grow up to resent her and not be able to have healthy relationships of their own. She talked and talked and eventually shared that maybe she was really worried that she would never be a witness for God ever again, because who was she to talk about God? Some people could hide their sins, but you couldn't hide divorce, you know? And how would anyone ever take her seriously when she had been through all of that?

After forty minutes she paused, her face was still hot but she wasn't crying. She was feeling passionate and angry again and she wanted answers, she wanted this woman to help her. She had probably articulated how she was feeling to this stranger better than she ever had to anyone else, and now she wanted to know how to make it better. She sighed. "I'm sorry, that was a lot."

"That was wonderful, Sadie."

"It doesn't feel wonderful."

"No, I'm sure it doesn't. But do you know what I just heard?" She put down her pen and notebook, she looked directly at Sadie. "I heard a woman who loves the Lord talk about how she feels like she has disappointed Him, how she wants to live for Him, and, how through all of that she mostly wants her kids to be ok. Is that a fair summary?"

Sadie pulled her head back. "Yes, yes I guess. But...but wait, why are you talking like that? Are you... a Christian?"

Dr. Marsden nodded slowly. "Yes, I am."

"I didn't want a Christian counsellor though." Sadie was stunned. "I *specifically* bypassed all of the Christian counsellors to find one who wasn't."

Dr. Marsden smiled. "Well, I guess God had other plans for you this afternoon."

"What?" Sadie's heart began racing.

"Sadie, I have been a Christian for all of my adult life. I don't advertise it through my work, but I have a very deep relationship with the Lord. I wouldn't be able to do this work if I didn't." She smiled then, "And I know for certain that if I wasn't, I wouldn't be sitting here with you right now."

"I don't understand."

"Well, I have a pressing feeling on my chest right now, telling me that God wants you to know how much he loves you."

"Stop, please." Sadie was crying now.

Dr. Marsden waited. She picked her notebook back up and sat back in her chair. She was filled with peace. This was why she loved her work. She was privileged to see glimpses of God's goodness. She waited for Sadie to finish crying before she continued.

"Sadie, you don't have to stay here if you don't want to. I have other counsellors that I can refer you to."

Sadie didn't know what to do. She was stunned. Eventually she found her voice. "Will you be able to help me though? I like you, but will you be able to help me without telling me to pray, or giving me a bible verse to read?"

The doctor laughed out loud, a sudden spontaneous laugh that made Sadie jump. "Yes." She chuckled again, "Yes, I can do that."

"Ok, then...let's do it."

Chapter Twenty Nine

Now

Friday night came in a blur and Sadie stood in her kitchen, opening and closing cupboards, re-checking that everything was still in the fridge. She caught herself pacing in circles and stopped, taking a deep breath. She had changed her clothes three times since she got home from work and had checked the clock for the hundredth time in the last hour. It was five minutes to six. She told Mason to come any time after six. What if for him, that meant seven? Or Eight? They were adults, nights out didn't have to start at the same time as they did for kids. She went back to the bathroom and checked her outfit. She had gone with a pair of baggy comfy dark green jogging pants, new ones though, and a tighter white V Neck t-shirt. She had kept her bra on even though it was a Friday night, unheard of, but she had *some* decency. She was comfortable but not frumpy. She tried to look nice, but she didn't think it looked like she had tried- not too hard anyway. She kept her makeup on, light as always, and her hair that she had straightened this morning was in a ponytail. It was still pin straight and fell down behind her back.

She moved to the downstairs living room and made sure the snacks were still there. Of course they were still there. She was the only one home. Who else would've eaten them in the last half hour? She scanned the family room and it looked fine, it looked great actually. She had done a deep clean that afternoon, bumping it up a day from her normal Saturday cleaning routine. She looked around again and didn't know why this all mattered to her so much. They were just hanging out, right? She couldn't let herself begin to like him again. She couldn't. Could she? Was it too late for that? Why was her heart racing? She told him she wanted to close the door so she could move on. Did she want to move on? Why did she say that? She was an idiot.

A light knock on the front door pulled her back to reality. She looked at the clock under the television, 6:01PM. She jogged up the stairs and opened the door, sticking her head out of the side first, making sure it was who she expected.

"Hi." Mason stood there. He wore jeans and a light blue button-down shirt over his broad shoulders, a white T-shirt underneath. He wore a dark blue ball hat, low over his eyes, and held a pizza box in one hand, a beautiful full fall bouquet of flowers resting on the top of the box.

She smiled and opened the door wider. "Come in."

He stepped into the entrance of her home and lifted the box and flowers. "For you."

"Thank you." She blushed and added, "You didn't bring any pizza for yourself?"

He laughed then, a wonderful sound that broke the tension. He looked around her home. "You have a great place here."

"Thanks," she replied. "Soon it'll be a little too small for us, but it's great for now. Come on in, I can give you a quick tour."

Mason removed his shoes and followed Sadie into the kitchen. He set the pizza box on the counter and asked her if she had any vases. She pointed under the sink, and he went to work, grabbing a vase, filling it with water, and after reading the instructions on the small packet of flower food, asked her where her scissors were. Sadie pulled them from a drawer and handed them to him. He added the water and flower food to the vase, trimmed the stems and arranged the bouquet in the vase. He swiped the remaining cuttings into his hands and asked her where the garbage was. Once the kitchen island had been cleared, he wiped it down and left on display in the middle was a beautiful bouquet of flowers. She looked at them, thinking of how beautiful they were, and how thoughtful it was for him to bring them. She looked over at Mason and he was staring at her. He just nodded. She didn't have to say anything.

She showed him around the rest of the upstairs and then they grabbed what they needed from the kitchen and headed downstairs to her family room. She had snacks and bottles of water set up on the table in front of the couch. He had brought down the pizza and a couple of plates, and she carried a bottle of wine and two wine glasses.

Sadie took a seat at the end of the couch and Mason took a seat on the other end. He faced her, but there was enough room between them that she felt comfortable. He began pulling apart the pizza and handed her a plate with a piece on it, opening a bottle of water and placing that in front of her as well.

"What service," she smiled. He shrugged but didn't say anything. She continued, "I'm glad you came tonight."

"Me too. Thanks for having me."

There was a comfortable silence between them, but there was so much she wanted to talk about and he seemed more pensive than relaxed.

"Kids made it off trick-or-treating ok?" He asked suddenly.

"They did." It was slightly unsettling, talking about that part of her life with him, but also, they were such a big part of it, there was no way around it. They were such a big piece of who she had become.

"Tell me about them."

Sadie paused and looked at him. He was sweet. She was remembering that now. He had always been sweet, but seeing it again in person, it was a lot for her heart. She pulled her legs up onto the couch and tugged down a blanket from behind her so that she had tucked herself fully into the corner. She saw him smiling at her as she did it.

"They're great." She answered. "Tess is a bit of a handful. She was born first, five minutes ahead of Jacob and is a big sister in every sense of the word. She's thoughtful. She talks a lot- it feels like too much most days. She has a couple of really great friends. She loves church, loves her family, adores my parents. Most days I think she loves me too."

Mason wasn't saying anything, just listening. He had settled back into his corner of the couch, but was so big that he took up not only his end, but crossed over into the middle as well.

"I'm not trying to be dramatic," she chuckled, "I think she's just had a harder time with Nick being gone than maybe the rest of us. Sometimes I think she blames me. I'm trying my best to love her through it."

"That has to be hard."

"It can be, but no harder than it has to be not having your dad around. I can't even imagine. She's in a dance class, and is really good, from what I'm told. She's in the Nutcracker in December and has a lot of practices for that right now... Jacob is... great."

"Jacob is great."

She smiled. "He has so much energy, he loves hockey. Eats, sleeps, breathes it. He was so excited that you were his coach... he doesn't mention Nick much, but I notice that sometimes he looks up and around the stands a lot when he has games, even though he knows where I'm sitting."

"I've noticed that too."

"So even though he might not say anything, I think he's hoping Nick shows back up, but he gives me no problems. He loves school, loves giving hugs. He's a good boy. I feel really lucky."

"That's awesome Sadie."

"You didn't want kids?" It didn't feel like too personal of a question to ask, it felt natural.

"I did. I do. Just have to find the right person, you know?"

She nodded, her face warmed. It seemed like as good a time as any to ask him what she wanted to. "Tell me about school, about the AHL."

"What? You didn't follow my rise to fame!?" He was laughing, but there was an underlying sadness that she could clearly see. He continued. "I got to BC and it was... great actually, if I'm being totally honest. The hockey part of it anyway. The guys on the team were awesome. One of the guys was hard on me, but I found out later that I had taken his spot in the first line. Griffin."

"Griffin Bean?"

"Beanie. Yup. He ended up becoming one of my best friends though, plays for the Red Wings now."

"Oh, I know of him. Jacob will freak out if he knows you're friends with him."

"Great friends. He still calls me all the time, no awareness of different time zones." Mason chuckled. "But yeah, the guys were great. I was playing well. I wasn't overly social really, kept to myself a lot." Mason was choosing his words carefully, Sadie noticed. "I was working towards an NHL contract. I wanted to finish school and get more experience in the AHL. In my last year I had a number of NHL teams calling me actually, but something never felt right about it. I think I was scared to sign on for such a huge commitment. I wasn't totally loving the lifestyle."

She couldn't help but think that he had been afraid to commit to her too. "I didn't know you were offered an NHL contract."

He chuckled. "A couple, one made a lot of sense for me. I only told my parents and asked them not to say anything. I ended up turning it down. I played for my team for another 5 years and then when I was aging out of the league, or at least when the team realized I wasn't going to be signing with an NHL team, they asked me if I'd be interested in coaching."

"And you took it."

"I did; but it still never felt like I was where I was supposed to be. I don't know, I know it sounds weird. Playing in the

NHL is every kid's dream, but that life of traveling all the time, sleeping in new beds, new hotels, being driven around in cars by people I didn't know, choosing food from menus all the time. It was... kind of lonely."

"I can see that... no girlfriend to keep you company?" She was genuinely curious.

"Sadie."

"What? I'm just asking. Clearly you know my story. I'm just wondering about yours."

"OK." he sighed. "I dated a little, yeah. I even brought a girl back here once. I wanted it to work, I tried to make it work, but it... it just didn't."

"Why not?"

He looked at her then, he wanted to make sure she truly heard him. "Because she wasn't you, Sade."

"Mason." Sadie flushed and she didn't know if her heart was ready to hear this. She put her head on her knees and took a second. She didn't believe him. She couldn't believe him. Was it suddenly really warm in here? Why did she have a blanket on her? She pulled it off her and placed it on the floor.

She had been talking to God non-stop since her counselling session on Tuesday and whenever Mason came to her mind since then, she pushed the thought of him away. She knew she was well on her way towards healing, but she still had a serious aversion to having her heart broken again.

If she let herself believe what he was saying, she would be opening her heart right back up for the taking.

"Sadie." She looked up again and he had scooted towards her, his knee now resting on hers. "I'm sorry if you don't want to hear it, but it's true. And I need you to know that. I actually saw your mom when I came home one time. She gave me a hug and it felt like I was home again, and after the hug I turned around to see my girlfriend standing there and my first thought was 'huh? why are you here?' I had wanted to see you. I had only ever just wanted to see you."

Sadie had always wanted clarity on what had happened between them, but didn't know if she wanted to know anymore. "You broke up with me Mason, you left me."

"I know. It was the biggest, stupidest mistake that I've ever made in my entire life. And I promise you that there hasn't been a day that I haven't thought about you, that I haven't missed you, that I haven't wanted what we had, back."

She wasn't mad, her voice wasn't raised. She was confused. "Then why didn't you just tell me that? I missed you too, obviously. You broke my heart. I spent years after we broke up trying to figure out what went wrong. Why didn't you just call me Mason?"

"I tried Sadie, I did."

"You tried to call me?"

"No Sadie. I tried to get you back. I showed up. I went back to Ontario for you."

Chapter Thirty

Then

Mason couldn't believe how stupid he had been. He was graduating this year with his business degree, he had received two different NHL contract offers in the span of one week, and the only thing he could think about, the only thing that made him want to get up in the morning was the thought of a life with Sadie Campbell. *Which contract would she choose? Where would she want to live? What would make her happy? What would make her proud?* When the thoughts had swirled enough that he couldn't even focus on his game anymore, when he began making stupid mistakes, he knew he had to go find her. He would beg her for her forgiveness.

Checking his schedule he was thrilled to see a bye week coming, no games or practices for eight days in a row, he didn't think twice and booked his plane ticket right away. A one-way ticket from British Columbia to Ontario. He didn't let anyone know he was going, what a great surprise it would be for their families, for him to return to Nova Scotia with Sadie this Christmas. He was almost giddy thinking about it.

The plane ride felt like it took forever, but catching a cab after he landed was seamless. He had reserved a hotel room a block away from the University of Toronto. The last time he was home he had pulled out his mom's address book and found Sadie's address. He saw the dorm room address crossed off and a new apartment address listed. She must be staying off campus for her fourth year, which made sense. He was excited to see it. He was excited about all of it. It was the first time in years that his heart felt like it was back where it belonged, and he hadn't even seen her yet.

Mason hopped in the shower and as he got dressed to leave, registered that it was 4PM local time. This was perfect, he thought. If she was home, he would beg her to talk to him, ask her if she would please go to dinner with him. He'd explain that he'd made a huge mistake and if she'd have him, he would do whatever it took to make her forget this time they'd spent apart.

He walked the block to her street, and finding her street number, walked to the front door. He didn't hesitate, he'd waited too long already. He knocked and waited for her to answer. After a few seconds, he couldn't hear anything inside, so he knocked again, this time harder. He was pulling at the bottom of his shirt when the door opened. It wasn't Sadie standing there though, rather a man. A grown man who looked like he had just gotten out of the shower.

"Hey man, what's up?" the stranger said.

"Oh, I'm sorry," Mason fumbled, his heart beating at double speed. "I was looking for Sadie Campbell. I must have the wrong address."

"No, this is Sadie's place. She's not home right now."

Mason was having a hard time processing why this man, wearing thick black framed glasses and a towel, was inside of Sadie's apartment. His mom hadn't mentioned that she was dating anyone.

"She's at her friend's getting ready for the Canadian Photography Gala tonight, she is accepting the 'New Generation' award. Brilliant work." He paused then, pushing his glasses up his nose, "Can I tell her who stopped by?"

"Uh... Mason. Mason Gray. I'm in town for a few days and was hoping to see her."

The man recognized Mason's name. He bristled and stood straighter. "Ah, the famous Mason."

Mason looked at the man. "Excuse me?"

"I know your deal, man. Sadie's high school sweetheart? The heart you *broke*? And now you're back because what? Because she's finally happy? Because she's winning an award?" He paused, "Because she's engaged? What is it?"

Mason grabbed the handrail to steady himself. "She's... engaged?"

"Yeah. We're engaged." He continued, "Tonight after the Gala, the one she's super excited about, I'm taking her out to celebrate. So, sorry, but I don't think she has time for visitors."

Mason stared at this guy. He couldn't believe this. Should he go find her, tell her he still loved her? Let her pick between him and whoever this dude was?

As if the man could read his thoughts, "I wouldn't bother. Sadie and I are really happy." He turned and grabbed a framed picture of the two of them off the table in the entry, showing Mason. "We're getting married this summer and moving back to Nova Scotia."

Mason couldn't look at the picture, he felt sick.

"I understand you're off playing hockey somewhere? Alberta?"

"British Columbia."

"Right... well, she doesn't want that, man. She's always talking about how excited she is to be going back East and I'm giving that to her. *I am.* As her *husband.*"

Mason nodded, stepping back from the door. "Right."

"Look. I'm sure you regret breaking her heart. I sure as hell would, but your time has passed. It's time to move on."

Mason had waited too long. Of course she was going to fall in love with someone else, of course someone would fall in love with her. She was... perfect. He nodded again and turned to leave.

"Do you want me to tell her you were here?" The man called as Mason made his way down the stairs.

"Nah, it's fine. I'm glad she's happy."

"She is."

Mason turned then. "Yeah, I got it. Treat her good, she deserves it. What's your name?"

"Nick. Nick Bell."

Sadie Bell? He hated it.

Mason walked back to his hotel, his hat was pulled low, hiding his wet eyes. The weight on his chest slowing him down.

Sadie had moved on from him. He hadn't ever truly considered that it would be a possibility, that she would be so happy without him. And how self-absorbed was that? Of course she wasn't waiting around for him, he had broken up with her, he hadn't stayed in touch. He could not be the guy that ruined her chance at happiness- again. He wouldn't do that to her; he loved her way too much. Unless God had other plans, he knew without a doubt that he was going to spend the rest of his life pining after his first love, Sadie Campbell.

Feeling like the biggest idiot, he stopped at the front desk to cancel the rest of the hotel nights he had reserved and went to his room to pack his bag. He called a cab. He wasn't even staying for one night; he had to get away from there.

At the airport he found a kiosk and booked his trip back to BC, the first flight he could find. He couldn't believe he came all the way here to find out that Sadie was engaged, that he had actually lost her. He held his emotion in until the plane took off, close to midnight. As the cabin lights went down, the tears fell, and Mason knew he would spend a lifetime regretting letting the best girl he ever knew get away.

Chapter Thirty One

Now

Sadie was shocked.

"What do you mean you came to Ontario? What are you talking about?" Her mind was racing, scanning those years and trying to remember. Nothing. Had he had one too many concussions? What was he talking about?

"Yeah, when we were in year four. I met Nick."

Sadie's body temperature was heating up again. "What are you TALKING about Mason!?"

Mason sighed and told her about that night, about his bye week, about the hotel reservation. He told her he showed up at her apartment and met Nick the night of the Gala when she was winning an award, about learning that she was engaged, and then, about flying back home.

"He never told me." Sadie said. She sat, stunned.

Mason wasn't surprised.

"Wait, you showed up before the Gala?"

"Yeah. I wanted to take you out, but when I found out about the award, and, well, and that you were getting married,

I wanted to respect that. I wanted you to be happy. It made more sense for me to leave. You were obviously happy with him, then. I didn't want to ruin anything for you, again."

She stared at Mason then, under the brim of his hat and into those eyes she used to steal glances at whenever she could.

"Mason, we weren't engaged then."

He reeled back. "What are *you* talking about? He said you were engaged. You got married."

"We only got engaged later that Spring. The night of the Gala we weren't engaged, we had only started dating the month before. The gala was in the fall. I remember. It was a long time after that actually before he proposed."

Sadie sat there staring at Mason. Neither of them could believe what they had just discovered.

"You came back for me?"

He looked over at her. He didn't want his anger to ruin their night, but he was SO angry.

"You weren't engaged?" He put his head in his hands. "I messed it up again."

Sadie watched him and she knew with every fibre of her being, that Mason Gray loved her. It was hard for her to reconcile that with what happened when they were younger, and it was also hard for her to regret the last 10 years. She had Jacob and Tess in her life. If she would've left Nick, she wouldn't have had them, and she couldn't imagine her life without them, but this. This piece of news changed things for her.

"I'm sorry." She said then, meaning it.

He turned to look at her, "Sorry for what?"

"I'm sorry that I didn't wait for you. I'm sorry that *I* didn't reach out to *you*. I was trying to protect my heart. I thought that you needed a break and that I would be bugging you, but I should have tried harder. I could have tried too." She didn't know what to do with herself. Where did this leave them?

"I don't want you to close the door on me Sadie." He said in earnest, "Please don't close the door."

"Mason."

He turned to look at her, to plead with her. "I'm serious. I'm the one who should be sorry. I was a stupid kid. That's what I wanted to say to you that night, and it's what I want to say now. I loved you so much and breaking up with you killed me too. I was trying to do what I thought was best for you, so you wouldn't lose your scholarship and so you wouldn't feel pulled away from your school and work, and so that you weren't spending all your free time trying to be with me and looking back, it just all seems SO dumb. We would have made it work. I know we could have. We could have been happy."

She felt like her bones were trying to jump out of her body. She was feeling unsettled and restless, but she couldn't move. She stared at him.

He looked sheepish. "I know. That was a lot... I'm sorry. Again."

And just like that a peace came flooding over her and she started laughing. "Oh my. It's so funny how God works."

"What do you mean?" Sadie looked comfortable, Mason thought now. She looked calm, and beautiful, and he remembered how he had always loved hearing her thoughts on everything, especially on God.

"I went to counselling this week."

"That's right. How did that go?"

"God showed up."

"He did?"

"Yep. It's a long story and I won't get into it all, but I hadn't wanted a Christian counsellor. I wanted someone to just help me fix how I was feeling, you know?"

"Yeah, I can see that."

"But as it turns out, she *was* a Christian. God pulled one over on me. She helped me start to work through some of the things I was feeling, gave me some homework, a book to read- and I realized on my drive home that if she hadn't been a Christian, in the end I probably would have ended up doubting all of the advice she'd given me anyway. Wondering what a Christian counsellor would have said. Always questioning what it was that God would have wanted from me, still struggling with knowing if he still loves me."

Mason was quiet, he hadn't realized the depth of what Sadie had been processing.

"But I've had some pretty great conversations this week and I'm not doubting that anymore."

"You're not?"

"No. I've realized that I was the one who decided to marry Nick. God didn't *make* me do that. Whether I felt like that was the right thing to do or not, it was my decision. He has given me so many blessings, and I've been trying to twist my mistakes into his punishment, and that's just not fair. He showed up through my dad this week, he showed up through Emily, he showed up through my counsellor. You're here tonight and I'm realizing so clearly that you've always loved me too."

Mason held his breath. He didn't dare hope.

"He keeps showing up for me, Mase. I need to stop pushing him away, and just start being thankful for what I have right in front of me." She looked at him, and he moved closer to her. He reached out and placed his hand on hers.

"I've always loved you... too?"

Sadie tilted her head, and shrugged, "Well, yeah. I don't know what you want me to say."

He stood and slowly pulled her up off the couch. He wrapped her in a tight hug, his frame completely covering hers. She could feel the laughter in his chest. He pulled back and held her small face in his big strong hands. He lifted his hat so she could see his eyes, "Sadie Marie Campbell. I love you so much. I have never ever stopped loving you. I left the AHL because God also showed *me* that my time there is over. I moved back to Darlings because you are here. I want to love you and take care of you, and help you love and take care of your children. I still want to be the man who makes you laugh and at the end of my day I want to hear all about yours on a porch swing. I want to go to church with you, and I want to watch you take pictures, and I want to know- I must know, that you will never *ever* again doubt how much I love you Sadie. I've loved you since I was a boy and I still want to love you when I'm old and grey. I've waited so many years to tell you... to be here with you, like this."

She looked up at him. "Mase."

He leaned down then and kissed her; he couldn't wait one more second. It started as a gentle kiss, but when she didn't pull away, he didn't either. He kissed her softly and slowly, their tongues finding each other again after so long apart. He placed one hand on the back of her head and the other on her back. He pulled her into him gently. He could feel that she wanted this as much as he did and his heart was soaring. She smelled so good, this woman he loved. He kissed her for a long time, the feeling of her in his arms making him unable to move. When she started to softly moan, he knew that he could no longer control himself and he pulled away.

"Is that too much for date one?" he asked lightly. His eyes were bright, burning with deep passion. Her cheeks were red, and her response came in a chuckle that warmed his heart.

"It doesn't feel like date one for me."

"Sade. It feels like date 1,000 and I need at least 1,000 more."

She wrapped her arms around him and held him tight. She couldn't believe he was here, in her home, with her. That he could kiss like that, that he still loved her like he did. His confirmation of that was more than her heart would have ever dared hoped for. His touch, the feel of his arms around her, had awakened her body. Feelings of longing replacing those of despair. She wanted more of him.

Having him here, so close, calmed her like nothing had since he used to hold her when they were younger. He was home. She didn't know now how she would ever let him go. Hugging him tighter as he rested his chin on the top of her head, she smiled into his chest, knowing that just maybe, she wouldn't have to.

Chapter Thirty Two

Now

Sadie sat in front of Dr. Melanie Marsden again, slowly rocking and waiting for her to ask her first question.

"Sadie. I'm so happy to see you again." Dr. Marsden began, picking up her notepad. "How have you been since our time together last month?"

Sadie smiled. "Really good. Well, mostly really good."

"Ok. That's wonderful! Why don't you start by telling me what's really good."

"Mason and I have been dating."

Dr. Marsden looked down at her notebook. "Mason, the boy you dated in high school? Who moved back to Darlings after leaving his hockey job?"

Sadie smiled, "Yes. Exactly."

"And how's that been going?"

"Really good." Sadie realized she was still smiling. She had been smiling so much lately. "He's really great. We're really great. His work is good, it's been a big learning curve for him but he's figuring it out. He's loving working with his dad, and we've been spending most of our free time together. I feel like a kid again. We're taking it slow, but we can't keep our hands off of each other." Sadie blushed.

"Always a good sign in a relationship."

"Yes." She was still smiling, "Work has been good for me too. I have a big event coming up in a few weeks and I'm excited about that. I'm working on a different show for the Spring and plans have been coming together for that as well. My team has been supportive. I'm being challenged but also feeling confident in the work."

"That's really great." Dr. Marsden paused, waiting to hear if more was coming. When Sadie didn't say anything else, she began again, "And things that are making life mostly good?"

Sadie stopped rocking and looked at the doctor. "I feel like I've been given this gift. Mason is back in my life, my energy has returned, and everyone in my life is supportive. Our parents cried when they found out we were back together." She laughed then, "Well, our moms. And we told the kids. We were going to wait longer to tell them, but it just didn't feel like a new relationship in the sense that we're not really worried whether or not it's going to work out or not. And we wanted to do some public things together, like go to church, and out for dinner, and Mason really wanted to get to know the kids better. We knew it was a big step, but we both prayed about it and last week agreed that we couldn't keep it from them any longer."

"How did the conversation go?"

"Mason and I talked to Jacob together at the rink one night after a hockey practice. I was waiting outside of the dressing room and when all the other kids had left, Mason called me in. Jacob was surprised to see me, but it was just the three of us. I asked him if he knew that his coach and I had used to date. He rolled his eyes and said that everyone knew that. We told him that we wanted to know what he would think if we started to date again." Sadie paused, remembering the moment. "He started crying. At first I thought he was upset about it, and I looked at Mason terrified, like 'what have we done', but then in all his gear, Jacob leaned over and gave Mason the biggest hug, before he even gave me one. He wiped his eyes and said that yeah, he was cool with it. Very cool with it. We laughed and hugged and it's been awesome with him. He and Mason are spending a lot of time together. If anything I miss each of them in a new way, but it's really good."

"And Tess? How did she take the news?"

"I talked to Tess on my own. Mason wasn't there. She was in her room and I knocked on the door and sat on her bed. I reminded her that I loved her and had promised to be truthful with her, and so I told her that on Halloween, the night that I had hung out with Mason that he had told me that he really liked me, and that he wanted to spend more time with me. I told Tess that I told him that I would really like that too, and she just said 'ok.'. We sat for a bit on her bed and I held her, because I knew there would be more, and eventually she had a few good questions 'would she have to call him dad?' Obviously, no. 'Would he move in?' No, that would only happen if we ever got married, and if that ever happened there would be way more conversations in between. She asked what would change, and I told her that he would hang out with the three of us more, and with me alone, and at larger family events. I told her he wanted to get to know her better, but only when she was ready, and she... well, she smiled. She was happy about that, I think. They went out last night for ice cream, just the two of them, and Tess was happy when she got back. She gave me a big hug, and all Mason had said was that 'it went really well, I told her how special you were to me.'"

"It seems like you both handled the conversations well."

"I hope so. We're trying. I'm praying non-stop, journaling again. Oh, how my journal entries are different." She paused, "But...I don't know. I'm still not feeling totally settled."

"Why do you think that is?"

"I don't know. I called Nick and told him that I was dating Mason. He didn't care. He's been dating someone for a while now I guess. He said he was glad I was happy. I believe him, so it's not that."

The doctor waited. She was good at waiting.

"I think I'm still feeling a little guilty maybe? For being *so* happy? Sometimes when I look at Mason, or the kids...Like, we were all at my parents together yesterday afternoon and everyone was talking and laughing and I was just feeling like something was off. So much of my life feels like it has been separated into pieces, and now that it's starting to come together, it's like I still can't forgive myself for getting here like I did."

Dr. Marsden nodded, like she completely understood. Sadie found comfort in that.

"Sadie, do you remember the last time we were together how you told me that on the morning of your breakup with Nick you had been looking at the pictures of your children on the wall? That seeing their faces made you sad for them, that you had struggled with raising them in a home with so much arguing, so much negativity and sadness? It was one of the reasons you had said you stood up for yourself."

"Yes, I do."

"Would you do that for them again?"

"Yes. Absolutely, yes."

"Would you do it for yourself, if not for them?"

"What... what do you mean?" She did do it for herself, it was why she carried the guilt.

"I want you to help me with something." She placed down her pen and notebook again, a signal, Sadie had come to realize, that she wanted Sadie's attention.

"Sadie, think back to when you were Tess's age, back when you were a little girl. Can you tell me what 10-year-old Sadie was like?"

Sadie sat back. She remembered running, and laughing, and playing in her yard. Her and Scarlett had spent hours and hours together playing Barbies. They had matching cabbage patch dolls that they dressed the same and had brought with them everywhere. "She was happy." Sadie said with conviction, though she could feel the emotion starting to bubble. "She was carefree."

"What did 10-year-old Sadie want when she grew up? Do you remember?"

Sadie closed her eyes, she thought of taking care of those cabbage patch dolls. "She wanted to be a mom. She wanted to grow up and be loved. She wanted to be happy."

There was silence and Sadie was waiting for another question, but it didn't come. She opened her eyes and looked at the sweet lady who sat across from her, who was now watching her.

"What would she say to you today? If she could reach out and talk to you?"

Sadie wasn't thinking of the 10-year-old Sadie now, she was thinking about that little 5-year-old girl who had been all smiles and staring up at her from her parent's photo album.

Sadie couldn't control the tears as they came. They welled up inside her so fast that she thought they had also captured her breath, she couldn't breath. She looked up at the woman across from her in fear, and in return she had been handed a tissue box. Sadie took a tissue from the box and began to cry into her hands, she had let that little girl down.

"I let her down." Sadie voiced, between sniffs.

Dr. Marsden sat back. "Did you though?"

"Yes, I got married to someone I shouldn't have, and spent years being so sad."

"No, Sadie."

Sadie looked up. "Yes."

"Sadie, I'm asking... what would that little girl say to you *today*."

Sadie thought about it again, understanding beginning to swirl in her chest.

"Probably... thank you for leaving."

The doctor nodded and continued, "And if I opened that door behind you and little Sadie was standing there? What do you think she's hoping for most of all, when she sees herself at 32?"

Sadie was crying again, "that she's... happy?"

The doctor nodded again and waited. "Can you do that Sadie?"

"I want to."

"Wonderful. We've determined then what your homework is going to be for this month."

"What's that?" Sadie wiped at her eyes.

"When you are doing all of the things you mentioned, the things that you know should bring you joy- being with your children, spending time with your family, seeing Mason... and you start to feel that guilt, I want you to think of little Sadie, because she is still in there, in you. Your homework is to live for her Sadie, to look at your circumstances through her eyes and try to experience it how you would want her to. If you want her to be happy, enjoy the moments, let her have that, let that piece that is still inside of you have that. You don't have to punish yourself any longer. You are also punishing that little girl, taking something away from her that she has always wanted. That is your homework."

"That's a lot."

"It is, and that's why it's called work. Because it is going to be hard work. It's changing the lens in which you view things, every day." She smiled then. "It's also fun. The world is hard Sadie, you know it and I know it. There are so many real things that we each deal with and go through, where looking at the positive isn't always realistic. But what you have now? A family who supports you, healthy children who adore you, a good man who loves you, a personal relationship with Jesus? Those are gifts Sadie, and they *are* the things worth celebrating."

Chapter Thirty Three

Epilogue

Jacob and Tess scrambled to get out of the car, excited to see their Grammy and Grampy to show them their report cards. They had graduated from grade six earlier that day and were looking forward to leaving elementary school to start Junior High the following September. A small graduation ceremony was held at the school for immediate family only and she and Mason had been there, clapping and cheering from their seats, a few rows from the front. He wasn't technically family yet, but no one said a thing as they made their way in together and sat down.

After the graduation, Mason had some things to do for his dad and so Sadie took the kids for ice cream before bringing them over to her parents, where they were hosting a summer kick-off party that evening. John and Judy and their family would be coming, generously supplying the lobster, and Stephen had hung twinkling lights over the patio tables that he had brought in for the evening's celebrations. The house was bustling and Sadie felt wonderful.

Her and Mason had been dating for about eight months now and she couldn't think of a thing that could be going better. She just wanted more of him, all the time. She had a suspicion that he would propose on their one-year anniversary. They had talked about making it through a full year of activities together, and she couldn't wait for next Halloween. Who would have thought? Tess had even asked a few weeks ago if her and Mason would ever get married, and when Sadie asked Tess what *she* thought about the idea, she had responded with 'that would be cool I guess.'

Sadie stood now in the entry of her parent's home and leaning against the doorway, watched her mom look over the kids report cards, commenting on their grades and reading aloud the nice comments written by their teacher. She watched her dad pass by the kids and secretly slip each of them a brown bill. They squealed and turned to him and Sadie smiled as he put his finger over his lips and told them to 'shhh', pointing to his wife, as if he was scared of their Grammy. They laughed and hugged him and then turned to hug their Gram as well, who smiled up at Stephen, knowing exactly what he had done.

Stephen shooed the kids outside to play, and then asked Sadie if she would take a walk with him over to John and Judy's house to pick up the tools they needed to open the lobster. She loved spending time with her dad and said she would love to. They had become even closer since their talk in his living room so many months ago, and she had swung by more than once to ask him his thoughts on different situations. He enjoyed being asked, though enjoyed spending the time with her more.

"I'm retiring in September," Stephen said as they made their way towards the path between their homes, "my time has come."

"Thats wonderful dad!" Sadie replied, slipping her arm through his. "I'm so proud of you! So happy for you." Then, as she thought about it more, "What are you going to do all day?"

He chuckled. "I'm sure I'll find things to keep me busy. The house needs some work; your mother would like to travel... Scarlett would love some extra help with the kids. And hey, I won't ever miss another baseball game."

Sadie nodded, "Sounds amazing. You feel ready?"

"I do," he said. "The work is hard, and we have a new sergeant at the detachment now, about 10 years away from retirement, so not a young buck. I have a really good feeling about him, and the team respects him. It's exactly what I was waiting for."

"That's great dad. Really great."

As they made their way down the path, she could hear the kids playing up ahead. They had grown up to love the frog pond as much as she did when she was younger.

"Mom! Come here!" Jacob yelled.

"Yeah mom! Hurry!" Tess called.

Sadie looked at her dad and smiled, "Do you think they caught a frog?"

"Not quite, but close." Stephen smiled. Sadie looked over at him, wondering what he meant. When he didn't make eye contact with her, she looked through the woods to see the kids sitting on the bench by the pond, but for some reason it looked like there were three of them. Who was with them?

As they rounded the corner, the full pond and wooden bench came into view. She paused as she noticed the same twinkling lights that had been hung in parents back yard had been strung around the pond, lighting it in a way that made the space feel magical.

Her dad removed her arm from his and as he stepped back, she heard another voice that she knew so well.

"Hi Sadie."

Sadie was frozen on the spot. Mason was now standing in front of her, looking as handsome as she had ever seen him. He was wearing a well-fitted suit she had never seen him in before, Tess and Jacob were sitting behind him on the bench.

"Mason?"

Mason laughed then, and nodded at her dad, who stepped around Mason. She looked behind Mason and past the bench. She couldn't believe how many people were standing on the path, their path. In the clearing next to the pond, she saw his parents, and both of her parents. Scarlett was there with Peter and her nieces. Mason's sister and brother, Jenny and Liam were there. Jeffrey from work stood next to Emily, who was full-on crying. Was that Rachel? Oh my goodness, Rachel was there, standing behind Jacob and Tess, who were smiling wide and sitting on the bench, holding hands.

"Sadie," Mason began, and stepped closer to her, his voice was shaking. He reached for her hands. "I know this is a lot. I couldn't let another day go by without asking you to be my wife because I've wanted to ask you for years. I have loved you my whole life, Sade. I don't want to make another plan, another decision that you are not a part of. I fell in love with you on this path, I know I did, and I wanted this to be the place where I made it official. I want to tell everyone I meet how much I love you and I wanted to start by doing it today in front of all the people who love you too."

Sadie started trembling and tears were falling from her eyes. They came faster as Mason let go of her hands and kneeled down on one knee. He looked back at the kids and winked, and they waved at him, grinning ear-to-ear. "I asked Jacob and Tess if this would be ok, and they've given me their permission."

She heard Emily sob from behind them, which made Sadie laugh while she continued to cry.

"Sadie Campbell. Will you and Jacob and Tess, will you become my family? I promise to love you and them, and any children we might have together, more than anyone else in the world, always. There is nothing in this world that would make me happier than being your husband. Will you do me the greatest honour of becoming my wife?"

Sadie looked back at her kids who were smiling wide and giving her the thumbs up.

"Yes Mason. Yes today, yes tomorrow, yes always."

Pump Up The Jam

Sadie's Teenage Mixed Tape

'Big House' - Audio Adrenaline
'The Great Adventure' - Steven Curtis Chapman
'I Will Be Here For You' - Michael W. Smith
'Home Run' - Geoff Moore and the Distance
'Flood' - Jars of Clay
'Shine' - NewsBoys
'Sunday School Rock' - Carman
'Baby, Baby' - Amy Grant
'Keep the Candle Burning' - Point of Grace
'In the Light' - DC Talk

Sadie's Current Playlist

'Kind' - Cory Asbury
'That's Who I Praise' - Brandon Lake
'Reckless Love' - Cory Asbury
'Surrounded (Fight my Battles)' - Michael W. Smith
'Yesterday is Dead' - Josiah Queen
'Won't Start Now' - Seph Schlueter
'Tubthumping' - Chumbawamba
        ^(Added by Mason, unbeknownst to Sadie)
'The Blessing'- Kari Jobe & Elevation Worship
'Made for More' - Josh Baldwin
'Gratitude' - Brandon Lake
'Goodness of God' - Jenn Johnson
'I Will Wait' - Mumford & Sons

Acknowledgements;

And a Personal Note from the Author

Writing a novel has been something that I have dreamt of doing since I was a little girl. I used to spend hours writing stories on pieces of white printer paper, folding them in half, stapling them, and drawing my own pictures to go along with my crayon printing. The fact that I can now hold in my hands a published novel of my own is more than I ever thought possible and I have people in my life that I would love to take the time to thank for helping me get here.

First and foremost, there would be no 'Returning Home' if not for an early morning in August of 2025 when God pressed this story on my heart so strongly that I had to pull over on the side of the road, find a napkin in my car console, and write it down. That morning, He gave me the first chapter and the last, and together we filled in the blanks. I still have the napkin; what a cool keepsake. While the novel that you've just read is not my exact story, the feelings of being mad at God and God in return fighting to get my attention, that is all very true. God has been with me through every stage in my life and for this book in particular, He is in every word, every chapter (and I think he's even ok with me using the word 'pissin'!). I hope that I have created something that He is proud of. Many thanks to God for entrusting me with these characters and with this story. I hope to be able to write more, always for Him.

This is my first novel, and so I don't have a publishing team, an agent, or someone who pushed me toward non-existent deadlines. What I do have is an amazing husband who, when I walked through my kitchen door that August morning and said, 'I know this is going to sound totally crazy, but I think God wants me to write a book', responded with, 'That's awesome, babe. Do it.' From there he has been by my side through early morning alarms and late-night writing sessions. I'd always break to watch the Blue Jay games (we came SOO close this year!), but the rest of my Fall has been working and writing, and I am *so* thankful for his unwavering support. Brian, year after year you've shown me, Ben, Megan, Mia and Averie what unselfish love looks like. I will forever be thankful that I am married to the person I like the most and who makes me laugh the hardest.

To my parents, Ron and Cindi Kelly, who were the very first readers of this book, and will always be my biggest supporters. Your faith in me and in this story means more to me than I will ever be able to explain. I love how much you checked in on me and how many updates you wanted. A girl will not find better parents.

To my sister, Erin Nickerson, and to my brother Jamie Kelly and sister-in-law Justine Kelly, thank you for reading and for your feedback. Erin, your suggested edits made the story better. Jamie, I miss you and appreciate you reading this romance novel, just for me. Justine, the text you sent me from across the country when you were done reading brought me to tears in the middle of a Winners, and forever and ever I will remember the love you've shown me and kind words you've sent me. You have been there through all of it, and I'm better for it.

To my group of girlfriends who love reading as much as I do and who made time to read this story and provide feedback on what I had written, thank you. Jessica Hudson, Jessica Cann, Rikki Jagger- your encouragement of my writing has meant so much to me, and your excitement for this book has added to mine.

To Pastor Brett Smith for praying for me, and for this book in your church office. Thank you. You are the first person to pray out loud for this book and the reach that it could have. The moment was impactful to me, making this venture seem both real, and possible.

To Mrs. Jayne Saunders, my grade six English Language Arts teacher, your faith in my writing has stayed with me for all of these years. I will never forget running into you years after I graduated from elementary school and you telling me that you hoped that whatever my future held, that it included writing. That's powerful. The influence teachers have on students should never ever be minimized. Thank you.

And lastly, to Aaron Chute, Megan Chute and Mia Chute- my world has been forever changed because of the three of you. Megan and Mia, though a fictional story, parts of this story were not easy to read. I have never, and will never, minimize the impact that divorce can have on the people we love the most- for me, that is the two of you.

Aaron, you are loved and will always be missed.

Would you like to talk about this book with other readers?

For suggested book club questions, please go to
christiemacdonald.ca

Find me on Instagram: @ChristieMac_Author

If you enjoy a story, the kindest thing you can do for the author is to share your feedback with others. If you feel inclined, please leave a review on goodreads.com, or on the site where you purchased or borrowed this book. Thank you for reading!